SPELL CHECK

BOOK ONE: THE TEEN WYTCHE SAGA

BY: ARIELLA MOON

SPELL CHECK

Book One: The Teen Wytche Saga

By: Ariella Moon

Visit www.ariellamoon.com

This book is a work of fiction. All characters, names, locales, and incidents are either the product of the author's imagination, or are used fictitiously. Any resemblance to actual events or locales, or persons living or dead, is completely coincidental.

Published by Star Tribe Publishing

Cover Design: AM Design Studios

Editor: Nia Shay

Print book ISBN: 978-0-9970554-7-4

*For Mackenzie Morison-Knox, Treasure Finder
and Barbara Cameron Kelly, who never lost faith*

Also by Ariella Moon

~ The Two Realms Trilogy ~

The Beltane Escape: Book 1
The Amber Elixir: A Two Realms Novella

~ The Teen Wytche Saga ~

Spell Check : Book 1
Spell Struck : Book 2
Spell Fire: Book 3
Spell For Sophia: Book 4

~ Short Stories ~

"Covert Hearts"

CHAPTER ONE

I can't remember how I got conned into this.

I remember Parvani saying, "Evie, I need you to buy me a spell book." I vaguely remember my mouth forming the word, "Okay." But I honestly don't remember what happened afterward. Maybe selective memory loss is one of the seven stages of grief.

I knew Parvani wanted to cast a love spell on Jordan Kent. She had a major crush on him, even though I'd told her he and I used to be real tight. Of course, I'd never explained *why* we'd had our falling out, or how I still thought about him every waking moment. And Parvani hadn't ever asked. She couldn't stop hyperventilating about him. Even I could see she barely registered on Jordan's radar. I mean, other than Honors Geometry and me, what did they have in common?

Hence her need for a love spell.

Parvani, who had at least three hundred dollars' worth of gift cards to major online booksellers, insisted an authentic spell book could only be found in a used bookstore. How she came up with this idea is beyond me. Maybe she'd watched too many episodes of *Charmed*. Anyway, the oldest, moldiest used bookstore ever was three towns away, and two blocks from my mother's favorite art supply store. Since Parvani's parents had every second of her life scheduled, I was stuck with the task.

As if I didn't have enough problems.

Parvani is my best friend and I had promised I'd help, so I hustled down Solano Avenue toward Well-Read Books. Warm pizza smells escaped through Paduano's Pizzeria's open door, making my stomach rumble. A homeless guy with bloodshot eyes jangled a paper cup full of coins at me. I warded him off with an apologetic shake of my head.

Tugging Dad's camouflage cap lower over my forehead, I opened the door to Well-Read Books and crossed the scuffed threshold. The glass door slammed shut behind me, frenzying a string of tiny pewter bells. I flinched, certain all eyes were upon me.

For a second my brain went on autopilot, taking in the cashier with her magenta Mohawk and silver eyebrow stud. The fluorescent bulbs humming overhead bathed her in a stark light. She stood behind the cash register, helping a bearded customer. The guy smelled like he hadn't changed his tie-dyed shirt since the sixties.

It would make a cool photo. I imagined where I'd crop the shot. Maybe I'd print it in black and white. It would look so noir if the only pops of color were the cashier's hair and the green dragon tattoo on her wrist.

Magenta Mohawk crossed her arms over the black muscle tee barely containing her cleavage, and threw me a what-are-you-staring-at look. Dad would have disarmed her with a grin and then taken the shot. But I'm not my dad. I'm not Dash O'Reilly, the famous photojournalist who'd gotten himself blown up in Afghanistan. I have his blue eyes, and before I'd expressed my grief and guilt with a cheap bottle of Intensely Autumn hair dye, I'd had his strawberry blond hair, too. But I'm nothing like him.

Magenta Mohawk narrowed her eyes as if she considered me a rival gang member or potential shoplifter. A hot flush fast-tracked up my throat. My gaze darted to the quickest escape route, the worn stairs leading to the basement where the occult books were shelved.

I fled past a display of political satire books and thudded down the steps. I paused on the second to last step and surveyed the room, the way Dad would if he'd just returned from a risky assignment. To my right, an organic-foods-and-expensive-sneakers type woman pulled a British travel guide off a high shelf. To my left, a shabby professor-sort thumbed through the record collection. *Hello, have you heard of a little thing called the twenty-first century?*

No axe murderers. No deranged homeless people.

I plunged ahead.

The reek of old books and damp wool permeated the basement. A super-cute college guy emerged from the medieval history section with a chocolate-scented designer coffee in one hand and a paperback copy of *Medieval Strongholds of Britain* in the other. He gave me an indulgent smile, like I was a kid or something.

Clearly I needed to convince Mom to let me wear make-up. Just because she didn't wear it shouldn't mean I couldn't. I'd only gotten away with the hair dye because Nana had bought it for me. Except for Mom, all the women in the Portland family either dyed or chopped off their hair when grief-stricken. At least I hadn't gotten a crew cut or gone purple.

I hurried past a hand-printed sign reading History of the Unexplained and headed for the section on magic. The books were shelved floor to ceiling — New Age, Earth Magic, Astrology. I pushed aside gloomy thoughts of being buried alive if an earthquake hit, and knelt on the yellow vinyl floor.

Under Wicca, I found *The Solitary Witch, The A to Z of Witchcraft,* and *The Circle.* I ran my hand over the colored volumes and closed my eyes. I willed my hand to stop over the right one. My fingers danced across several books, slid across a slim volume, moved on to the next, and then slid back. *Pick me!* the book seemed to scream.

I opened my eyes. *Teen Wytche.* The slick paperback cover was the exact same shade as my chipped, Perfectly Plum nail polish. I tapped the new-smelling book against my unpainted lips. Somewhere behind the wall, an ancient heater rumbled to life and the vent over my head spewed warm air. A spicy scent evoking stews cooked over campfires and colorful horse-drawn caravans wafted my way.

A fast scan of the book's table of contents assured me there was a section on spells. Still, I scooted two feet toward the Pagan section. *Sacred Stones. The Goddess Within.* Still clutching *Teen Wytche,* I trailed my fingertips over volumes with titles printed in medieval-looking script. My pulse pounded like ancient drums.

"Evie?"

My heart catapulted to my chin. "Mom! You scared me."

"Sorry." The woman is five-foot-six and walks like a panther. I've thought about tying a bell around her neck, or making her wear high heels. And makeup.

"Did you find anything for Parvani?" she asked.

"Yes." I held up the spell book. "It's for history class. She's doing a report on witchcraft."

Mom arched one eyebrow. She seized the book and flipped through it, pausing when a passage caught her attention. Her mouth tightened. She leaned closer to the page and her dark red hair tumbled across her shoulders. I flinched when she snapped the book closed. A pained expression haunted Mom's eyes, and I was sure she'd say no.

Instead, she handed me the book and cleared her throat. "Do you want to check out the photography section?"

"No!" Heat rushed to my cheeks. What if we encountered Dad's book with his photo on the back, with him holding his camera and wearing his lucky cap? My legs melted into string cheese. *I'm not ready to look. I can't. I won't.* Because no matter what the grief counselor said, it was my fault Dad had died. Which is why I don't take pictures anymore.

Mom frowned. She still wore Dad's emerald on her left ring finger — it glinted under the fluorescent lights. "Honey, you're the photo editor. Miss Roberts said you're going to flunk Yearbook if —"

"I said, no."

"Fine." Mom's eyes bulged with exasperation. "Let's pay and get out of here."

I didn't argue.

We made our way up the stairs and around a half-dozen circular display tables. Mom stopped and righted an upside-down display book on urban herbology. I spotted the magazine rack. Shay Stewart, Hollywood's bad boy, smirked at me from the glossy cover of *Kiss*. His disheveled dark hair alluded to a late night and subsequent reluctant tumble out of bed. His pouty lips begged to be smooched. My lower abdomen fluttered.

"Wait."

"Evie." Mom drew out my name like a warning. She scowled at the magazine, then read the cover lines aloud. "Five beauty tips that work! Channel your inner goddess! Shay Stewart in the flesh!" Her eyebrows knotted. "I don't think…"

"Please, Mom. I have my own money."

"All right." She handed me a jute reusable bag. "Just hurry up and pay."

"Yes!" I gave her an air kiss, then hustled over to the cashier. Magenta Mohawk must have gone on break, because an older woman laden with rings, bangles, and necklaces, and wearing a colorful headscarf rang up my purchases. When she took my money, our fingers touched. An odd crackle zapped up my arm.

The crone threw me a sly look as she dropped the book and magazine into the jute bag. She wagged a gnarled finger and warned, "Be sure to read every word." Her voice rasped as though it had been pulled from the earth like a weed.

Gulping, I nodded.

She leaned closer and her musty breath breached the space between us. "Good luck, dearie."

The warm caravan scent blew over me again. The bells on the front door tinkled. I twisted toward the sound, the fine hairs on my nape standing on end. No one was there.

I snatched the bag, rushed to Mom, and slid my arm through hers. "Do me a favor?" I pushed the bag into her hand. "Will you carry this?"

She hesitated. "Okay."

"Thanks." I glanced back at the checkout counter. The odd clerk had vanished. Magenta Mohawk was back on duty.

CHAPTER TWO

Parvani's red turtleneck peeked out from beneath her green mesh gym shirt. The color combo looked sort of Christmas-y, though I didn't think Buddhists celebrated that particular holiday. Below the Wildcats logo emblazoned in white letters on the oversized jersey, Parvani had inked her last name, Hyde-Smith, with a black sharpie.

"Can you believe this rain?" she said in her clipped, I-lived-in-London-for-five-years way.

"At least it means no mile." We prayed for rain every Friday, the cursed day the cafeteria served soggy tacos and every kid at Jefferson had to run a mile in physical education.

Parvani surveyed the crowded gym. "Look. There's Jordan."

Jordan had added blond highlights to his curly brown hair. As if he didn't attract enough attention with his easygoing smile and lake blue eyes. *Unfair. He gets highlights, and I can't even wear Soft Fawn eyeliner.*

Parvani's expression morphed from annoyingly love struck to scarily determined. "Did you find a spell book?"

"Yes." *And I can't wait to get rid of it.* "Did you bring your sleepover stuff?"

Parvani angled her head toward the corner where she'd left her bulging backpack.

Mr. Willis blew his whistle. I screamed.

Dread and embarrassment blazed like a wildfire across my cheeks. I scanned the quieting throng. Had anyone heard me? Okay, *everyone* had heard the scream, but how many knew it had come from me? Before Dad died, I'd never been this high-strung.

I pulled his hat lower over my eyes. My gaze flicked on Jordan. He held a basketball over his right hip as he walked toward us, his mouth set in an easy smile. As he neared, Parvani gasped.

Jordan shifted the ball to his left hand and squeezed my shoulder. "Hey, Evie. You okay?" The heat from his hand sent a cozy warm river rushing toward my belly. My mind blanked.

"She's okay," Parvani answered for me.

Tweet! Coach Willis spit out his whistle. "Free play, people. Grab a basketball, volleyball, or soccer ball. Get moving!"

Jordan released my shoulder and dropped his hand back to the ball. His gaze embraced both of us. "See ya." He trotted off with his annoyingly perfect gait and joined some of his football teammates near the basketball hoop.

Parvani's eyes were wild behind her ebony designer glasses. "Jordan Kent spoke to us!"

I shook myself. "Parvani, I've known him since preschool."

A basketball bounced off my shin, and with a flash of pain I joined the game. Our wet gym shoes squeaked as we pounded across the polished floor. Balls thudded. Students shouted. The nose-crinkling stench of sweat soured the air. I got caught up in the din, the blur of bodies, and Parvani's frequent glances at Jordan.

Finally, the bell rang. The sharp bounce of basketballs eased, replaced by the ragged breathing of twenty-five freshmen. Parvani retrieved her backpack. The thick strap pinned her long black hair to her shoulder, but she didn't seem to notice.

"Meet you at three," she said, breathless.

"Won't I see you at lunch?"

"Right. Of course." Looking dazed, Parvani dashed off to Honors Geometry without a backward glance.

I'd never qualify for an advanced math class. Before Parvani had moved to town two years ago and taught me some math tricks, I couldn't even memorize the multiplication table. Who knew when you multiplied any number by nine, the answer would always add up to nine? Eight multiplied by nine equals seventy-two. Seven and two equal nine.

I bet Jordan knew. Maybe he would have told me if the Smash Heads, his football teammates and the vilest bullies in the school, hadn't teased him until he quit helping me. *The loser.*

I headed to a class I did excel in — Spanish. Afterward, I shivered across campus to Mr. Ross's classroom. Parvani and I had taken video production from him over the summer, so now he let us hide out in his room during lunch and watch *Bewitched* reruns on television.

"*Hola,* Mr. Ross."

He glanced up from the quiz he'd been grading and frowned. "Evie, don't you have a raincoat?"

I adore Mr. Ross, but sometimes he sounds way too much like my mother. "My sweatshirt is fine."

"Cal Bears?" he asked, reading the logo.

"Yeah. My dad went to the University of California at Berkeley." *Before — you know.*

"I see." He sighed, his stocky body seeming to cave in on itself. "Well, close the door. I'm trying to keep the heat from escaping."

"Sorry." I pivoted and bumped into Parvani. Water ran off her expensive umbrella and onto my striped toe socks. Zhù Wong, one of Parvani's fellow math geeks, appeared beside her and blinked at me from behind his rimless John Lennon glasses.

"Evie, Ms. Ravenwood assigned tons of math for the weekend," Parvani said in a rush.

There went the sleepover.

"I'm going to the library and see how much I can finish. Want to come?"

Zhù's eyes widened in a silent plea. *He should just tell Parvani he likes her. It's so obvious.* Well, not to Parvani. She was too preoccupied with Jordan.

"Pass." I raised my chin. "Math makes me break out in hives."

Zhù's shoulders relaxed. He'd grown four inches over the summer and his weight hadn't caught up with his height, giving his long face a chiseled look. He might look hot if he ever smiled.

"Cross the field together after school?" I asked Parvani.

"Sure." She radiated relief. I should have been offended, but we both knew she had a better chance of preserving her A average and getting to sleep over if I didn't distract her. "Bye, Mr. Ross."

He waved like a parade queen. "See you, Parvani."

Zhù followed Parvani, turning toward me at the last moment with his hands together in a prayer position. With his back to Parvani he mouthed, "Thanks," and gave me a little bow.

Okay. Maybe he doesn't have to smile to look cute.

I closed the door behind them before I returned to my desk. *Bewitched* already played on the television. I scowled at the actor playing Darrin, the witch's mortal husband. His no-witchcraft-in-my-house attitude irked me.

I slumped onto the molded plastic chair and pulled my copy of *Kiss* from the middle compartment of my backpack. The magazine should have had a slick, possibly toxic smell. Instead, a faint spicy scent clung to it. A tingle spider-walked down my spine as I recalled the strange crone in the bookstore.

The wall clock ticked. Three hours and fifteen minutes until the last bell. Three hours and forty-five minutes until I could unload the spell book on Parvani and be done with the creepy thing.

The rest of the afternoon went by in a blur. I tuned out in Math, kind of hid during Yearbook, and spent Biology trying to ignore Jordan, who sat in front of me. *A hex on teachers who make students sit in alphabetical order.*

When school ended, I met up with Parvani and Zhù at the edge of the field. Zhù was saying, "It was so worth it."

"What?" I asked as we headed across the soggy grass.

Parvani shook her head. "He used British spelling on the vocabulary test in English. On purpose!"

Zhù shrugged. "Hey, solidarity. My way of protesting her marking you down when you did it last week."

"But I slipped up. You did it on purpose and it cost you half a grade."

"So what? I made my point."

"I think it was a sweet thing to do," I said. "Insane, but sweet."

Zhù beamed. *Wow. His teeth are so white and even.*

Ahead and to the right, the field dipped a bit. Rainwater had formed a glistening miniature lake, where a flock of gulls waded, searching for worms. Watching the birds, I paid little heed to the whip of nylon windbreakers and the masculine murmur behind me. Had my internal Smash Heads Radar been on like it should have been, scarlet warning lights would have flashed.

Tommy Deitch and Evan MacDonald pushed past us. Tommy shoved Evan, knocking him into me. Our shoulders collided hard, like an SUV sideswiping a mini electric car.

"Hey!" I halted, pain shooting down my arm.

"Tommy! Evan!" Jordan yelled from what sounded like several yards behind us.

They ignored the edge in Jordan's voice and ran for the tiny lake. The birds took flight, their snowy wings thrumming the air. Evan, his greasy copper hair flying, jumped into the puddle. Icy rainwater splashed my jeans.

I loathe being cold. I especially hate being cold and wet. Ignoring the squelch of running feet behind me, I concentrated on Evan's pale, mocking face.

"Grow up, Evan." Then I flung a forbidden noun at him, one my mother would never, ever approve of, just as Jordan trotted up alongside me. Tommy laughed. Evan's jeering expression caved as if I had hurt his feelings, which kind of shocked me. Parvani gasped. I'd like to think it was from the testosterone fouling the air, or Jordan's belated appearance, but since she was glaring at me, I guess not.

Jordan, clutching a football, raised his arm. "Go long!"

Like well-trained dogs, Tommy and Evan took off toward the road, where parents picked up the freshmen and sophomores who didn't take the bus. *Maybe if Jordan throws the ball hard enough, they'll both keep going — into oncoming traffic.* A twinge of remorse struck me. *I take it back.*

Jordan hustled after them, turning once to wink at me. My heart bungee-jumped. My stomach fluttered like hummingbird wings. Jordan caught up with the Smash Heads long before the gate, and grabbed each one by the shoulder. "Be cool," I heard him say as he herded them toward the cyclone fence.

"Sophisticated language, Evie," Zhù said.

"Shut up."

"Evie!" Parvani's voice rose.

I worked my fingers across the bruise forming on my bicep and gritted my teeth against the cold seeping through my jeans. We reached the cyclone gate.

"See you Monday, Parvani." Zhù angled his body away from me and locked his gaze on the path.

Parvani patted Zhù's shoulder. "Bye." She drew out the word. Sympathy tinged her voice.

Regret fireworked through my insides. "Zhù —"

He'd already slid through the gate like a wounded shadow and disappeared into the throng of kids milling about the sidewalk.

Parvani swatted my arm. "What is wrong with you?"

"I'm sorry I yelled at Zhù. I'm mad at the stupid Smash Heads, not him."

I leaped across the muddy path, squeezed through the half-open gate, and stormed up to Mom's battered Volvo. It wasn't too hard to spot in the line of newer BMWs and SUVs. All the other parents had left their cars running to keep the heat blasting. Not my mom. Not Miss Save-the-Environment. I opened the car door and hurled my backpack onto the floor mat. My breath formed a vapor cloud as I scooted in. Mom slid sideways in the driver's seat and lowered her romance novel. "Bad day?"

"I'm drenched and freezing."

"Oh. Bummer."

"Hello, Ms. O'Reilly." Parvani slipped into the back seat beside me. A small stream dribbled off her umbrella and onto my sneakers. The cold water seeped through the canvas, through my socks to my skin, and I swear it pooled around my bones.

"Hello, Parvani." Mom faced front again and rotated the key in the ignition. Welcome heat blasted from the vents, and Chicago blared from the stereo. "Wishing you were here…"

Mom tensed and flicked off the radio. I knew the song reminded her of Dad. I held my breath, hoping she wouldn't burst into tears. She sniffed as she eased into traffic behind a monstrous blue SUV. "How about hot cider and popcorn in front of the fire when we get home?" Her voice sounded a little strangled.

Parvani threw me a worried look. "Brilliant."

"Yeah, good idea, Mom."

The windshield wipers whooshed across the glass. Mom's suggestion did sound good, especially if I could change into dry socks and sweats first. I relaxed against the gray leather seat.

The rearview mirror reflected Mom's green cat eyes. "You girls have any special plans for tonight?"

Parvani clutched my wrist.

"Nah." I tried to sound innocent and nonchalant despite the sudden spike in my pulse rate. "Just the same old stuff." *Witchcraft, casting spells, voodoo…*

"Uh huh." Her eyes narrowed in the mirror.

An uneasy feeling festered in my stomach. Maybe I should have skimmed the spell book before I'd bought it. *What if something goes wrong? What if we screw up and accidentally summon a demon, or burn down the house?*

Or worse, what if the spell actually works?

CHAPTER THREE

Baby, my retriever mutt, picked up her filthy tennis ball and wagged her tail when she saw us.

"How are you, Baby?" Parvani, who isn't allowed to have pets and thus has no idea where Baby's mouth may have been, sank to her knees and let Baby lick her face.

"No French kisses," I admonished Baby. Then to Parvani, "Be right back."

I grabbed a pair of flannel pants and a dry sweatshirt, and ducked into the hall bathroom. While I changed, the rose-colored toilet made an irritating running noise. Dad had always promised he'd fix it "next week." I blinked back the sudden rush of tears and expelled a long breath. "Think about something else," I told myself.

My gaze scuttled to the gray broken floor tile near the sink. The night before Dad's funeral, Nana had dropped her hair dryer on it. She had flown up from Palm Springs to lend us moral support. The weird thing was Mom had seemed angry with her, as if somehow Dad's death had been Nana's fault. Nana may be a little airy-fairy sometimes — okay, a *lot* airy-fairy, but she's hardly the type to fly to a war-torn country and plant roadside bombs. Besides, she'd always liked Dad. Still, Nana had acted a little guilty, as if she *had* done something.

Maybe Teen Wytche *has a clarity spell.*

I plunged a burgundy terry towel between my toes, stabbing at memories and guilt. Afterward, I pitched the towel in the hamper and shuffled back to my bedroom, where the homey smell of popcorn and cinnamon apple cider greeted me.

"Your mom brought us a snack," Parvani called out from the rag rug in front of my desk. Baby's head nestled against her thigh, suspiciously close to the snowman popcorn bowl perched on her lap. "I love your house."

"You're crazy. It's a forty-year-old fixer-upper. You live in a mansion."

"My house is like a posh, soulless hotel." Parvani swept her hair up into a low bun and shoved a pencil through it. "A wing for each of us so no one has to interact."

"You can always slum with us." I grabbed an overflowing handful of popcorn. Baby snapped to attention and hunted down the rogue kernels.

"Thank you." Parvani glanced around. "Where's the spell book?"

"It's here somewhere." Since the crone cashier had freaked me out, I had left the grimoire in the bag and hidden it under last year's math binder. I fished out the jute bag and hefted it.

"What's the matter?"

"It's heavier than I remember." I pulled out the book and flipped it over in my hand. "Whoa."

Parvani sat up straighter. "What?"

"I could have sworn it was a paperback."

"It looks like purple leather to me."

"Plum," I corrected, running my fingers over the raised silver lettering. "I'm *sure* it was a paperback."

"Now you're the crazy one." Parvani wiped her hands on a cloth napkin. "Let me see."

"Take it," I said. "It gives me the creeps."

Parvani stood up and handed me the popcorn bowl. She cradled the book in her arms, her dark eyes sparkling behind her designer eyeglasses. She picked her way across the debris littering my floor. "Cool title. *Teen Wytche.*" The air whooshed out of my down comforter as Parvani plopped belly-down on my bed and started flipping through the pages. "Hmmm. There are a lot of steps we have to take before we can cast a spell."

"What's this 'we' stuff? I just agreed to get the book."

Parvani went all injured-puppy on me and pursed her lips. "You have to help with the spell."

No, I don't.

"Come on. Please?" Parvani furrowed her perfectly waxed and shaped brows.

What I should have said was, "Look, I've had a crush on Jordan since we were three and I'd rather you didn't go after him." Instead, I thought about how Parvani had saved my butt in math about a million times, and how she'd stood by me even after I'd dyed my hair Intensely Autumn.

I sighed. "Can't we just skip to the magic words and wave a wand?" *Then bury the book in a cemetery or something?*

"Thank you!" Her gleeful expression morphed into a frown. "But I don't think so. We have to prepare ourselves and your room." She trailed her hand down the page. "Do you know anything about casting a magic circle?"

"I used to draw chalk circles on the driveway." *With Jordan.*

Parvani glared over her black frames.

I faked nonchalance. "Maybe we should just forget the whole thing."

"Hmm." Parvani wrinkled her nose and kept reading.

I sank into the beanbag chair. *This could take a while.* There's a reason Parvani was in Honors Geometry and I wasn't. She never skips a step. She also reads much more slowly than I do, so I knew better than to try and read over her shoulder. Instead, I rooted through my desk for a highlighter. I know Parvani. She loves to highlight.

"Thanks." Parvani took the yellow marker and pushed up into a sitting position. She immediately popped the top off and highlighted a sentence. "We have a problem."

"What?" I asked.

"You have to be calm and focused to perform magic."

"Okay. So what's the problem?"

"Evie, you are the jumpiest person I know."

"So not true." I hunkered into the beanbag, rustling invisible beans.

Parvani flung me a look.

Okay, maybe I have become a little edgy since Dad died. I popped another handful of popcorn into my mouth and ground the kernels between my teeth. *Dad had no right chasing photos or destiny or whatever in such a dangerous place. Maybe if he had loved Mom and me more—*

"We need a serene setting." Parvani glanced at the piles of old school papers, magazines, and books on my desk. Her gaze darted to my unmade bed, and then swept over the wet sneakers, rank sweatshirts, CDs, and a nest of discarded belts heaped on the floor. "Your room could use a bit of *feng shui.*" She pulled a *Teen People* from a pile at the foot of my bed and held it up. It featured Jessica Simpson wearing an *I heart Nick* tee shirt.

"Okay, that can be recycled. But you're the one who wants to do magic. Let's go to your house." I could just imagine her horror if I drew a chalk circle on her celadon silk carpet.

"My brothers would never leave us alone. It has to be here."

The Terrors, her younger twin brothers, would be harder to get rid of than my piles of junk. "Okay. I'll pick up while you figure out what to do."

Parvani's smile crinkled her eyes. "You're the best." She straightened into a lotus position, her perfect posture reflecting the years of ballet she had taken before a stress fracture forced her to quit. Highlighter fumes fouled the air.

I clattered together a mountain of dusty CDs and slid them into a metal holder. Parvani winced at the scraping noise, so I switched to gathering up clothes. Hopefully, she didn't notice the underwear from the discount department store nosedive when I threw the heap into the hamper. I shoved the tangle of belts into my white wicker hutch. A wallet-sized photo fell out through one of the cracks on the side. The handwritten caption on the back read: Jordan, Age six, First Grade. I turned it over and stared at his gap-toothed grin.

Behind me, the highlighter screeched across the page. I stashed the picture under the belts, then cleared the floor and the spare bed, tossing most of the stuff in the closet. The house phone rang, its insistent buzz cut short after the second ring. *I hope I get a cell phone for Christmas.*

Parvani was still reading, so I picked up my copy of *Kiss* and flipped to the article on the Goddess. *Look inward and awaken your inner Goddess.*

"The editor from *The Times* is on the phone," Mom said from the doorway.

I gripped the magazine so tightly it crackled and bent. "Tell her I can't talk right now."

"She wants to know if you're ready to start taking photos again for the school section. There's a game this weekend at Campo. What should I tell her?"

"Tell her no. I'm not ready."

Mom ground her teeth. I knew what she wanted to say. I needed to get back on the horse. Or we needed the money, since Dad had never been able to get life insurance. Or I needed to move on, so she could, too.

Well, I can't.

Parvani kept her head down and scribbled notes on binder paper. Mom sighed and left. I flipped back to the goddess article. *Envision what you'd like to experience.* Seeing Dad again? Making peace with Jordan? My heart tightened. Taking photos...?

"Don't you have one of the Goths in your English class?" Parvani asked.

I lowered the magazine. An image of a short girl, whose oversized black tee shirts hung on her thin frame, leapt to mind. "You mean Salem?"

Parvani blinked twice.

"It's what everyone calls her since she crossed out 'Remember The Alamo' on Tommy Deitch's notebook and scrawled 'Remember Salem'."

"We need to text her. Where's your Jefferson High phone book?"

Doing spells in the privacy of my own room was one thing, but texting a *Goth?* My voice cracked. "I don't even know her real name. She's Sarah something."

Parvani stood and plucked a lime-green booklet from the wreckage on top of my dresser. "We'll find every Sarah in the ninth grade. You must have heard her last name when Mrs. Knapp called roll. We just need to jog your memory."

"I'd rather jog in a hurricane without my sweatshirt. Didn't you hear? In the fifth grade, Salem put a hex on Britney Bauer, and Brit broke out in hives the next day."

Parvani lowered the directory. "Total coincidence."

"No it wasn't. Even the Smash Heads are afraid of her. Why do we need to text her?"

"We need lots of props to cast a spell, and I don't know where to buy them."

Sheesh. Judging from the pentacles and other exotic stuff Salem wore, she would be the best person to ask.

Parvani skipped through the pages of the school directory. "Sara Douglas?"

I shook my head.

"Sarah Grimes?"

"No."

"Johansen? Mackenzie? Miller?"

I drew in a quick breath. A shiver shimmied down my spine.

Parvani's stare bored into me. "Miller? She lives on Lucas. Is she just down the street?"

I felt as though the warden had given me truth serum. Against my will, my head bobbed up and down.

"Let's go see if we can spot her," Parvani suggested in her most reasonable, don't-worry-this-won't-hurt-a-bit voice.

I glanced out the window. "Are you insane? It's raining."

"Then text her."

I began to reconsider Parvani as my best friend.

"Come on," she pleaded. "Baby would love to go for a walk."

Upon hearing the W-word, Baby bounded across the room, stopped at the threshold, and glanced back at us with an excited expression. Now I *had* to go. "All right. But it will be dark soon, so we'd better hurry."

Wild-eyed, Parvani grabbed her umbrella and gray sweatshirt. "Where is your leash, Baby?" The L-word sent Baby racing toward the front door. Parvani sprinted after her.

"If we don't see Salem on the street, we turn back," I insisted.

Parvani already stood outside, her umbrella up, the amazing patchwork scarf she had designed herself wrapped around her neck. She did a *grand jeté* over the primroses while Baby, a quick shadow behind her, zigzagged after a scent.

Mom met me at the door. "Where are you going?"

"Parvani said the W-word in front of Baby. So we're going to walk around the block, maybe go as far as Lucas." *You know, pay the neighborhood Goth a little visit.*

The wind stirred Mom's auburn hair. "Okay. Just be back before dark."

"No problem."

Baby barked at me from the end of the drive. I lifted her leash from the wooden peg. Then, before my better sense could stop me, I walked out the door, cold rain stinging my face.

I could almost feel the hex hives erupting.

Chapter Four

Baby, happy and stinking of wet dog, pulled me eastward toward Lucas Drive. Parvani bumped alongside me in a valiant effort to hold her expensive wind-battered umbrella over our heads.

"No way will Salem be out in this."

"She's a Goth," Parvani replied. "She probably thrives in miserable weather. You know, the sky is filled with angst…"

Yeah, right. A rain-heavy willow grabbed at the umbrella as we rounded the corner. Plaid nylon dipped in front of my face, blocking my view of the street. A foot in front of me, Baby stopped and tensed. *Please don't let it be Salem.*

An unholy yapping broke the silence, followed by a somewhat familiar voice yelling, "Einstein, shut up!"

Parvani tilted back the umbrella, affording me a clear view of a tiny, black-clad, windswept figure. *Salem.* I'd know those scary kohl-lined eyes and short black-and-purple hair anywhere. My heart sank to my Perfectly Plum toenails.

"Hey!" Parvani waved and shouted up the street.

Salem's cockapoo yapped louder, a feat I would have thought impossible, and strained to break free of its leash. Salem squinted at us like a bounty hunter in a futuristic movie. The question "Friend or foe?" was etched on her pale face, which, I noticed for the first time, looked kind of delicate and pretty beneath all the Goth makeup and the I-can-kill-you-with-a-curse attitude.

"I see you got dog duty, too," I called.

"Yeah." Salem sounded resigned. "It's my sister's dog. She left him behind when she went off to college." The rain matted Salem's razor-cut hair to her skull. "Einstein, be quiet!" The repulsive beast sat at Salem's feet and growled.

Parvani nudged me in the ribs.

"This is Parvani Hyde-Smith," I told Salem. "I don't think you two have any classes together."

Salem shook her head. "Sarah Miller."

"I've seen you around." Parvani stepped forward, forcing me to follow or get soaked. "I noticed you wear a lot of unusual jewelry," she gushed in the tone she uses when she's trying to talk her dad out of money, or get a sales clerk to call another store for her. "Where do you shop?"

Salem squinted again, sizing up Parvani, probably searching for a hidden insult. Or worse, maybe she was concocting a hex. It didn't take a shrink to see she had major trust issues.

Parvani's tact was failing, big time, so I tried. "Parvani is interested in crystals, and…" I searched my mind. What else had the book mentioned? Wands? Brooms?

"My cousin is into New Age stuff, and I want to send her a birthday present," Parvani added.

Einstein jumped up and barked, the little lie detector. Salem stared at Parvani so long, Parvani's hand on the umbrella started to quiver. Maybe it was just from the cold.

Salem shifted her gaze to me. "Try Sage Mage on North Broadway. It's across from the skate park where all the loser jocks hang out."

Parvani's mouth tightened, and I knew she was thinking the same thing as me. *Jordan practices there.*

Black eyeliner ran down Salem's rain-slick cheeks, giving her a vampirish look. She tugged on Einstein's leash. "I better get him inside."

"Sure. Thanks." I met Baby's gaze. "Let's go."

A small gale pushed us homeward. Baby splashed through the gutter, oblivious. We were almost home when Parvani said, "Your friend helped us a lot."

"Salem's not my friend. I hardly know her."

"Anyway," Parvani continued, "tomorrow I get a break from BMCR."

"BMCR?"

"Building my college résumé. My service project has been postponed because of the rain, and I don't have piano until one o'clock. So I'll ask my mother to take us to Sage Mage."

"All I have is two dollars."

Parvani puffed. "We're talking about *my* mother."

"Right." One thing I know about Mrs. Hyde-Smith — she's never flinched at a price tag.

"Let's make a list of everything we'll need." Parvani wore her project face.

"Wouldn't it just be easier for you to talk to Jordan?"

Parvani threw me a withering look.

"Or not." Maybe I could watch a Shay Stewart movie while Parvani did her research.

***

The next morning, after a breakfast of granola and orange juice, Parvani and I were waiting in the entry when horrible news arrived in a shiny new Lexus. Her father, Dr. Hyde-Smith, sat behind the wheel, and the Twin Terrors were in the back seat.

"Oh no," Parvani moaned. "Mom must have gone to the spa."

Mrs. Hyde-Smith was what Nana would call a high maintenance woman. Parvani liked to compare her mother to Buddha — when he lived lavishly in a palace and had yet to gain enlightenment.

The cracked entry tile crunched behind us. "Is there a problem?"

I jumped. "Mom, quit sneaking up on us!"

Parvani thumped her forehead against one of the narrow vertical windows flanking the front door. "Dad's driving. Now we'll never get to go to Sage Mage."

Dr. Hyde-Smith stomped out of the car. Water from yesterday's rain still beaded the car's waxed hood. Being a dermatologist in a town filled with teens paid well.

The twins started slugging each other.

"I'll take you," Mom offered.

Parvani hugged her. "Oh, thank you, Ms. O'Reilly."

"Let's check with your dad." Mom opened the door before Dr. Hyde-Smith could ring the bell.

Parvani launched herself at her father. "Dad! I just remembered I have to buy some stuff for Social Science. It's due on Monday."

I rolled my eyes. *Right. Social Science.*

Muffled shouts sounded from the back of the Lexus. Dr. Hyde-Smith scowled at the twins. "Not now, Parvani. I have to take your brothers to get their hair cut. Maybe later."

"I have piano later."

"I can take the girls," Mom said. "When would you like Parvani home?"

Parvani's dad tapped his fingers against his thighs. "I may be a while with the twins…"

"Why don't I keep Parvani for an hour or so and then drop her off by noon?"

"Please, Dad. This is my only morning off."

"All right," Dr. Hyde-Smith relented, pulling out his wallet. "Here, you'll need some money." He peeled off two twenties and handed them to Parvani.

"Thanks, Dad!" She kissed his cheek and snatched the bills from his hand.

Mom and I exchanged a look. I would have to clean out the dishwasher, make my bed, and help make dinner for two months to earn forty dollars.

"See you later." Dr. Hyde-Smith squared his shoulders, exhaled, and then headed for the car.

Mom closed the door behind him. "Does this have something to do with the book you two bought?"

My cheeks heated, but I nodded.

"I thought it was for History."

"World History," Parvani clarified. "It's listed under Social Science."

Mom gave her a hard look. "Okay. Get your sweaters while I find my purse."

Oh, goodie, a field trip.

"I'll grab the list," Parvani said.

I followed her into my room and retrieved my sweatshirt from the floor. Beneath it, Shay Stewart smirked at me from the cover of *Kiss.* My gaze darted to the hot pink teaser, "Channel Your Inner Goddess!" *Well, Goddess, Parvani has her hopes up. Now what?*

An odd tingle tiptoed down my arms and I could have sworn I heard the tinkle of tiny pewter bells.

CHAPTER FIVE

I pushed open the glass door to Sage Mage and the cloying stench of incense assaulted me. I wondered how long I could hold my breath and stave off an allergy attack.

"Oh, I love this place." Parvani swept past a rack of Wicca and New Age magazines and headed for a velvet-draped table. "Look, they have Buddha." She patted the seated sandstone figure as if it were an old friend. "We could use one of these for our God symbol."

"We only have forty-two dollars. The book said you could use a candle or horn instead of a statue. Either one would be a lot cheaper."

Parvani frowned. "You're right. We better see what the rest of the items cost, then decide."

I took the list from her hand. "What are Quarter Guardians?"

"They represent Air, Fire, Water, and Earth."

Whatever. "Well, according to this, we can use flat stones, candles, and even a feather. There are flat rocks down by the creek. We could use them."

Parvani blinked at me as though I were a genius. I guess her family had never had to cut coupons or count pennies. I studied the list some more. "Parvani, you can't burn incense in my room. I'm super-allergic."

"Sorry. I forgot. Do you think the spell will still work?"

I was pretty sure it wouldn't work no matter what we did. Actually, I *hoped* it wouldn't work. Since Parvani's brows were scrunched with worry, I said, "I'm sure it will be fine."

She pushed a quick breath out her nose. "I'll search for a red candle for love — *unscented* so you won't have an allergy attack — the wand, and the knife. You find a Goddess symbol and a pentacle." She handed me a separate list she'd written on a neon green sticky note. "See if they have any of these stones. They are supposed to have magical love properties." Parvani headed for a pine case filled with smelly candles. I didn't hold out much hope she'd find an unscented one.

I glanced at Mom. She lingered by the counter, chatting with a clerk who had the quiet, knowledgeable air of a librarian. To Mom's right, half hidden by the counter, was a small corner where the magic rocks lay waiting.

I walked past a loud trio of girls who plucked dangling earrings off a Plexiglas display case. Beyond them, a skinny, twenty-something guy examined dragon figurines. A father, mother, and young daughter crowded around the three-tiered pyramid display of rocks and minerals.

The little girl picked up a translucent rock, palmed it for a few seconds, and then returned it. I watched as she rounded the pyramid. The stones had been divided by type, with each group nestled in a tidy round basket marked with a hand-printed sign. The girl bent over a mound of tiny, amber colored stones, plucked one from the heap, and weighed it in her palm.

"This one," she said.

"Excellent." Her father beamed. "Citrine. Good for emotional balance and for quick relief from nightmares. Your sister will be most pleased with the results." He patted the girl on the shoulder, then herded her toward the cashier. The mother gave me a nod as she strolled after them.

I stood alone with my list and stared at the shoulder-high display.

"It works best if you let the stone pick you."

Startled, I glanced up from a cache of rose quartz into the kind eyes of the librarian-like saleswoman. My gaze darted. I spotted my mother at the opposite corner of the store, her back to me as she examined some expensive-looking crystals in a glass cabinet.

"Look at each grouping," the clerk said. "See how some attract your interest and others repel it?"

My glance slid across moonstones, amber, some white lumps with no sign, and petrified wood. No reaction. Fool's gold. Iron pyrite. Agates with fossils. *Nada*.

On the top tier I spotted a nest of fire-colored topaz, and my heart skipped a beat. I reached for one, changed my mind, and plucked another from the pile. Cradled in my hand, cool and smooth, it seemed happy. It was home.

The clerk's eyebrows arched a good half-inch closer to her hairline.

"This isn't on my list," I said.

"The list is for your friend. The topaz is for you. It is what *you* need."

The small sign read: Topaz. Two dollars. My heart lifted. Surely Mom would spring for the tax.

I handed her the list. "Which of these stones do you think will be best for attracting love?"

The clerk glanced at Parvani, who discussed black-handled knives with a college-age saleswoman wearing a nose ring and a turquoise sari. "I'll have Serena show your friend the stones."

"Thanks. Where can I find pentacles?"

The woman pointed to the counter closest to the door. "They're scattered among those cases. I'll be happy to pull out any of the trays for you to look at. By the way, I'm Wenn."

"Evie." I thanked her again and headed off.

Mom met me at the counter. "Any luck?"

I thought of the orange topaz, now warm in my hand. "May I borrow some money?" I showed her the stone. "I have the two dollars, but I need help with the tax."

"Did you pick this out?"

"It sort of picked me. I wish I knew what its magic properties are."

Mom twisted her emerald ring. "Topaz gives you courage. It dispels fears and gives you peace of mind." She mustered a wan smile. "I'll buy it for you."

"For sure? Thanks!" I gave her a tight hug. Mom's lips curved upward, the closest she'd come to a happy face since Dad had died.

The door opened, and a bone-chilling wind preceded a frizzy-haired woman with a bad dye job and a worse scowl. The New Age CD playing on the sound system skipped. A sour, evil smell scythed through the incense-laden air. I clutched the topaz and slipped my other hand around my mother's arm. Mom drew herself erect. Her green cat eyes glittered and narrowed.

Wenn met the newcomer near a display of tarot cards. "Madrun. The object you ordered is in the back. Would you care to examine it in private?"

The woman raised her chiseled jaw. Wenn must have interpreted the gesture as a yes, for she motioned toward the back of the store. "This way."

Madrun followed her like an ill wind. The two headed toward a couple of aisles of bookcases I hadn't noticed before. To my surprise, Salem emerged, saw Madrun, and ducked behind a shelf.

Halfway across the store, Madrun halted and angled her pointy chin toward Mom. Madrun's lips tightened, then sadness flashed in her eyes and she acknowledged Mom with a small nod.

Mom stiffened.

Rebuffed, the woman's feral gaze shifted to Parvani. Maybe she could smell Parvani's 50 SPF sun block over the incense.

"Mi-Miss Ravenwood," Parvani stammered.

Madrun Ravenwood stared down her long nose at the items gathered in Parvani's arms. "I thought I gave you enough math homework to keep you busy all weekend, Miss Hyde-Smith."

"You did," Parvani said in a rush.

Out of the corner of my eye I saw Salem sneak behind the candle display, drop low, and then head toward the pyramid of magic stones.

"Then why aren't you home?" Miss Ravenwood demanded.

"I worked during lunch on Friday so I…"

"Don't fool with things you know nothing about." Acid laced Miss Ravenwood's voice.

Parvani shook her head like a bobble doll. "Yes, ma'am."

Miss Ravenwood jerked up her pointy chin. Her glance flicked to Mom and me, and then she disappeared after Wenn.

Serena, the sari-clad clerk, appeared at Parvani's side. "Don't let her frighten you. Come on, I'll ring these up for you."

Parvani's hands shook as she placed a knife, a pink crystal, and a pink candle on the counter.

Crap. I was supposed to find a Goddess symbol.

"All the red candles were scented, so I hope this pink one works," Parvani said as Serena rang up the items. "The knife is pretty expensive. How did you do?"

"Not too well. I was about to look at the pentacles." I glanced toward the rock display, but Salem had vanished again.

"Thirty-two dollars and ninety-six cents," Serena said.

Parvani thrust the two twenties at her. "Forget the rest," she told me. "Let's just get out of here."

"Okay."

Serena handed Parvani her change and her bag.

"Wait a sec." I set the sweaty topaz on the counter.

"And this." Mom placed a small, drawstring pouch beside it. She paid for both, then slipped the topaz inside the moss-green velvet and handed it to me.

Parvani's glance swept the back of the store before she headed, nearly sprinting, to the front door. I speed-walked after her, clutching the pouch like a talisman. Mom followed at a dignified pace, her shoulders back. Her emerald glinted as she flexed her fingers. For the first time since Dad's death, she appeared ready to rumble.

CHAPTER SIX

"Can I leave this stuff at your house?" Parvani asked as the Volvo bumped along her costly cobblestone driveway.

"Sure." My thoughts lingered on the skate park across from Sage Mage. Maybe Jordan had been there, practicing with the other boarders. I forced myself to focus. "Don't let Miss Ravenwood freak you out."

"Miss Ravenwood picks which students get placed in AP Calculus. I can't get into Cal Tech or M.I.T. without it."

"I thought you wanted to go to design school."

"College is over three years away," Mom soothed. "Besides, your test scores and grades will help decide your placement."

"Maybe. Thanks, Ms. O'Reilly." Parvani opened the car door, dragged out her backpack, and eased the door shut behind her. Rushing past the trickling Tuscan fountain, she waved as the housekeeper opened the front door.

I pulled the topaz from its velvet pouch and ran my thumb over its smooth surface. I wished the rock could bestow peace of mind. My thoughts burned like overexposed film. As much as I didn't want Parvani to perform the spell and steal Jordan, I hated to see a math teacher scare her. Bad enough they'd intimidated me my whole life.

Whoever thought up those seven stages of grief forgot one. Indecision. Massive indecision. If I ever have another session with the grief counselor, I'll ask her about it.

Mom made quick work of the few blocks and two socioeconomic levels separating our house from Parvani's. Back in the unfamiliar cleanliness of my room, I took another look at the list. We still needed a wand, a Goddess symbol, a God symbol, Quarter Guardians, and a pentacle. I decided to be a supportive friend and gather all the objects I could. Then I'd leave the rest to fate, although fate hadn't done me any favors lately.

I headed for the entry and yelled, "Mom, I'm taking Baby for a walk."

Mom emerged from the kitchen, a chocolate-splattered *Kiss the Cook* apron tied around her waist. "Be careful."

"I'm just going to the creek." *Not the war zone.*

I grabbed Baby's leash and darted out the door. A cool breeze gusted down Lucas Drive as Baby and I hurried toward the stream beyond Salem's house. We reached the low, undeveloped hills and followed a deer trail through wet, thigh-high foxtails. A covey of nervous quail scurried across the damp path ahead of us, then took flight.

Breathing in loamy earth smells, I followed the sound of running water to the muddy creek bank. Baby splashed in and out of the stream while I found four flat stones to use as Quarter Guardians. The rocks were the size of teacup saucers, but thick and heavy. I dropped them into Baby's unused poop bag and prayed she wouldn't make an unauthorized pit stop on someone's lawn.

"I have to try harder in Gym," I told Baby as I swung the rock-laden bag over my shoulder. The Quarter Guardians thumped me in the back. Evidently, they agreed.

We hiked back to the sidewalk. Friday's storm had littered the ground with branches and wet clumps of leaves. Baby stopped under the weeping willow and sniffed a fallen limb. I tugged on her leash, but she nosed the branch and refused to budge.

"Come on, Baby Girl. These rocks are heavy." Who would have thought magic would be such hard work?

Yap, yap, yap! Salem emerged from behind the tree with her wretched beast. "Interesting way to carry a poop bag." Her lips, painted congealed-blood red, twitched. I lowered the bag in front of me. Salem gave it a quick glance then said, "Thanks for not giving me away at Sage Mage."

"No problem. Do you know Miss Ravenwood?"

"She's my geometry teacher. She taught my sister, too." Salem rolled her eyes. "So what were you and Parvani up to?"

"Nothing. Parvani was shopping for her cousin."

Einstein barked.

The frost crept back into Salem's voice. "Of course she was." She tugged on Einstein's leash and started to walk away.

"I'm sorry. I've had a bad day. Can we start over?"

"I'll think about it." Salem leaned forward to pet Baby. Her silver necklace dangled in the air between us.

A pentacle! "I realize we hardly know each other, but do you have a spare pentacle you could loan me?" I asked. "I promise I'll give it back."

Salem fingered the encircled five-pointed star and squinted. "You don't look like the pentacle type."

"I'm not. Let's just say there are extenuating circumstances." *Like Parvani going insane.*

Salem dropped her voice to a conspiratorial whisper. "Are you and Parvani creating a sacred circle?"

"No." Technically, it was true. Parvani wasn't even here. "Of course not."

Salem sized me up. I shifted from one foot to the other. Then Salem's attitude changed and she angled her head to one side. "Your dog wants you to take the wand."

My gaze flicked to the narrow tree limb. "It's not a wand. It's a stick."

Salem jammed her hands into the pockets of her crimson Massachusetts Institute of Technology sweatshirt. It kind of shocked me to see her wearing something other than black. "Suit yourself," she said. "I gotta go. By now Amy will have called."

"Amy?"

"My sister, Miss Perfect. Captain of the girls' water polo team, president of everything in high school, and now, star college student."

"Best thing about being an only child," I said. "No footsteps to follow."

"You're so lucky." A weird expression passed over her face. "I'm sorry. That was stupid."

"What do you mean?"

Salem drew in her shoulders as if she wanted to conjure up a hole and fling herself down it. "I meant, you know, because of your dad."

"Oh." For a second, I'd forgotten the whole school knew.

"I saw his photos in *Time* once," Salem babbled. "He was awesome. No wonder you're the photo editor for Yearbook."

My throat constricted and hot tears rushed to my eyes. I crouched and picked up the willow stick so Salem wouldn't notice. "I better go do my biology homework."

"You're taking Biology? I thought only tenth graders took bio."

"Parvani is taking it." *And Jordan and Zhù, so basically, everyone I know.*

"You have to be awesome in algebra to take it as a freshman. Amy took it then, but I decided to wait until next year, even though I'm pretty good at math."

The sick feeling I got whenever I knew a math test was coming up fast-tracked through my intestines.

"You okay?" Salem asked. "You don't look so well."

"I think there's been a mistake."

"About bio? You might still be able to switch classes."

"Maybe." Humiliation scorched my cheeks. There must have been something about math ability in the Biology course description. I must have skipped it. But Parvani wouldn't have. She'd probably highlighted it.

"Don't you have the Smash Heads in Gym?" Salem asked.

"Yeah. Unfortunately. Why?"

"Keep your guard up. I heard we start Capture the Flag next week."

"Are you kidding? How middle school can you get?"

Salem fluffed her bangs. "This is Coach Willis's first year teaching high school. He's from some middle school down south. I don't think he's made the adjustment yet."

"Great." I pictured the weeks of torture ahead and grew queasier. I knew the Smash Heads would take me prisoner, or I'd trip over one of the orange cones dividing the field. *I so do not need this.*

I hoisted the Quarter Guardians over my shoulder. By some ill magic, they seemed twice as heavy.

CHAPTER SEVEN

Thanks to some major rain Sunday night, the field was flooded on Monday, and we couldn't play Capture the Flag. When Gym ended, Parvani rushed off to Miss Ravenwood's class.

As I trailed Parvani's wake, someone tapped me on the shoulder. I readied for a Smash Head sneak attack, but came face to face with Jordan. Staring into his blue eyes felt like skinny-dipping in Lake Tahoe at Christmastime. The shock stole my breath.

"Hey," he said.

I shouldered my backpack. "Hey."

He glanced around, as if making sure no one could overhear us as we walked toward the door. "Does your mom still belong to the women's service club?"

A pang of grief rose from its pine box and stabbed me. "No. She quit after Dad died."

"Oh. I'm sorry."

"It's okay." We stepped out into the cool autumn air. I pulled the front of my hoodie up to my nose. "Why? What's up?"

"I remembered one of their philanthropies helped seniors." His voice trailed off. "I couldn't think of its name."

"Contact Care."

"That's it." His lips pressed together and his eyes glistened.

I stopped and placed my hand on his forearm. "Is this about your grandpa? Is he getting worse?"

Jordan nodded, then pressed his hand against his lips. "I gotta get to class." His voice caught. "Bye."

"See ya." Regret washed over me as I watched him hurry off to Honors Geometry, his shoulders hunched as if he carried a burden far heavier than his backpack.

Coward, I scolded myself. I should have given him a hug.

Memories flooded back of all the times Jordan's grandpa had taken us to get ice cream or see a movie. Funny, I didn't have as many memories of Jordan's parents — they had always been at work.

My chest constricted. Dad had died without warning. One minute we had our lives ahead of us. Birthdays. Christmas mornings. He had wanted to walk me down the aisle if I ever married. Then he was gone, and the grief slammed me like a bus without brakes. But at least he had been Dad until his last breath. Could Jordan's grandpa still remember birthdays or holidays? How much longer until he forgot his children's names or that Jordan is his grandson?

How does Jordan do it? Hide his despair. Function like normal. Convince people like Parvani he's easy going, without a care.

I've heard of "aha" moments. Instead of a light bulb illuminating above my head, a blinding strobe light flashed. Jordan had trusted me enough to ask for help. And I was going to let Parvani steal him away with a love spell?

No way.

I entered Spanish fueled with righteous determination, and scored a hundred percent on the pop quiz. The sun came out during lunch. My mood continued its upward trajectory until I remembered I still had to go to Algebra.

I slunk into the classroom and hid in the back row, my thoughts confetti. *I have to stop Parvani. I can't let her perform the spell just to spite Miss Ravenwood.*

The sharp screech of chalk drew my attention to the front of the class. Mr. Bentley—former Marine drill sergeant, now math teacher to the numerically challenged—scratched algebraic equations onto the blackboard. I prayed he wouldn't call on me.

Finally the bell rang, and I raced out into the crisp air. I fought my way through the backpack-wielding crowd toward Room 222. Yearbook.

"Evie!" Parvani squeezed past a pack of popular girls and drew up beside me. "How was Algebra…?"

Zhù Wong walked a few yards ahead, his back to us. Tommy Deitch cut in from the side and bore down on Zhù like a rogue SUV. Before Parvani or I could call out a warning, Tommy slammed Zhù against a large, metal trashcan. Zhù hit with a loud bang. A startled sophomore cursed. Tommy laughed. Parvani hissed air between her teeth.

The potential for a fight or major humiliation hung in the air. Even a clutch of popular girls stopped talking and watched. I expected Zhù to fall like an overturned turtle. But somehow he landed on his feet, his body tense. Tommy gaped. For a wild second I thought Zhù would do something amazing, like flatten Tommy with a karate chop or a *taekwondo* kick.

You could have heard a sheet of binder paper drop. Zhù stared Tommy down. Zhù. The Nerdinator. Zhù, who weighs half as much as Tommy.

"Whatever." Tommy shoved his way through the throng, headed straight for us. I clutched the topaz in my pocket. "What are *you* staring at, Jekyll and Hyde?"

My mind stuttered.

"Ow!" Tommy swerved away from the jab of Parvani's umbrella. "Watch it, Hyde." Scowling, he stormed off, holding his side.

"Jerk!" Parvani tucked her umbrella under her arm, then dashed after Zhù. "Are you okay?" she asked him as I headed up the ramp to Yearbook. "You were awesome."

My teacher, Miss Roberts, poked her head out the door. Short and plump with shoulder-length, flyaway hair, she appeared closer to fifteen than twenty-three. "What's going on?"

As much as I would have loved to see Tommy hauled off to the office, I followed the unwritten No Snitching code. "I'm not sure," I lied. "Someone must have banged into the garbage can." In the back of my brain, I relived the scene. Tommy's startled face would have made a great photo. *Too bad I don't take pictures anymore.*

"The first set of pages is due October fifteenth," Miss Roberts reminded me.

Forty-one pages in nine days? No problem. There were two other photographers on the staff — Zhù, and an artsy sophomore named Hallie.

"Hallie is sick today," Miss Roberts said. "You'll have to shoot the fashion candids."

"But…"

"I'll do them." Zhù joined us on the ramp. I so wanted to hug him.

"I need you to cover academics. So grab your cameras, you two, and get going. Be back before the bell." Miss Roberts made a sweeping gesture and whisked us into the classroom.

Zhù retrieved the digital cameras from Miss Roberts's desk and handed one to me. It felt cool and heavy in my hand. My mouth went dry.

"Let's hit the classes together," Zhù suggested.

The room silenced. I didn't have to glance around to know the rest of the class was staring. "Miss Roberts…"

"Go on, Evie. You'll be fine."

Sweat gathered beneath Dad's lucky cap. I wanted to scream, "I can't!" But Miss Roberts ushered me out the door.

Zhù talked me down the ramp. "Parvani has French. Let's start there."

Hot tears brimmed my eyes. *I hate Miss Roberts. I hate Yearbook. I hate Hallie for missing class.*

Zhù walked me past the library then guided me to Room 505. *"Parles-tu français?"*

I glared. *Can't he hear my heart pounding? I may die right here on the spit-covered concrete.*

"Right. Well, *plié* and *pas de chat* are about all the French I know. If you live in California, you should speak Spanish. *¿Es verdad?"*

"Sí," I replied. *French ballet terms? Zhù's been hanging around Parvani way too much.*

Zhù opened the door. Madame Marseille raised a penciled brow. *"Oui?"*

"We're here from the yearbook." Zhù nudged me.

The room smelled of chalk and strawberry lip-gloss. I tore my gaze from Parvani in the third row and cleared my throat. "Zhù would like to take some candid shots of you and the class."

"And Evie needs to take a few students outside for fashion photos," Zhù added.

Evan MacDonald scraped back his chair, stood, and put one hand on his hip. His copper hair hung in oily strands down to his jaw. "Take me. I'm fashionable."

I sneered, remembering all the recesses in fourth grade when he and Tommy had held me prisoner. Parvani thought Evan had a crush on me, which proved she wasn't as smart as she looked.

"Perhaps you would like to pick someone else," Madame said in her thick accent.

Zhù slipped from my side and started photographing Parvani. She designed most of her own clothes, and always wore something interesting.

"You, you, and you." I pointed to a black-clad Goth who seemed like he needed an escape, one of the preps who would probably be mad she'd missed class time, and a pixie-like brunette I recognized from middle school.

Madame sighed. *"D'accord."*

Zhù circled Parvani in full ninja-paparazzi mode. I left him and trooped outside.

"Could you make this quick?" the prep said.

I grunted. My heart raced. I had the weird feeling I had separated from my body and was walking beside myself. Maybe the photo shoot was happening to someone else.

"Why don't we pose around this?" The Goth halted beside a smooth-barked tree and swung his lanky frame up into its V-shaped fork.

"Perfect." The brunette sprite sat at the tree base, her skinny legs hugged to her chin.

"Fine." The prep leaned against the trunk and flashed a tight smile. "Just get it over with."

The camera weighed against my palm like a small, silver corpse.

"Dude, take the picture."

I fumbled for the shutter button. It had to be there. Why couldn't I find it?

You can do it, Evie. It sounded like my father's voice, calm inside my head. *Remember, I showed you how.*

I can't breathe. I'm going to die right here and have to haunt Jefferson High for eternity.

"It's okay, Evie." The familiar scent of 50 SPF sun block registered in my brain. A warm hand eased the camera from my clammy grip.

Parvani. Thank goodness.

Parvani held the digital to her eye. "Hold it another second."

It took me a few turbo heartbeats to realize she meant the students around the tree, not me. The camera clicked.

"Okay, got it. *Merci.*"

"Is she all right?" the pixie asked.

"Could you tell Madame I'm going to take her to the nurse?"

"Sure, dude."

"Parvani?" Zhù appeared beside her. "Wow, Evie. You look like you're going to faint."

Parvani handed Zhù the camera. "Tell your teacher Evie isn't feeling well, okay?" She slipped her arm around my waist. "Come on, Evie. Let's go to the office."

Someone who sounded like me said, "Okay." It might have been me. With my heart roaring in my ears, I couldn't be sure. The phantom weight of the camera pressed against my palm as Parvani led me toward the glass-fronted office. Jordan emerged from the boys' bathroom and we almost collided.

Jordan said, "Hey…"

Parvani shook her head and propelled me forward.

I told my heart to slow down. Then, maybe, I could hear my father again. But my pulse kept racing, and all I could hear were Jordan's footsteps as he fell into step behind us.

CHAPTER EIGHT

"Just rest, sweetie." Mom tucked a fuzzy blanket around my neck. Its woolly moose motif marched across my shoulders. I sank into the sofa and watched the flames curl around the pressed log in the fireplace.

Mom walked to the far end of the sofa. As she sat down, a scrap of blood-colored corrugated paper fell from her sweater. I recognized the tatter. It wasn't from Mom's line of handcrafted greeting cards, our "bread and butter" between Dad's royalty checks. She had started a series of large collages after Dad had died. The latest was of a headless woman fashioned out of red corrugated paper. The lower half of her body was a gold-leaf clock.

I don't want to think about the symbolism.

"I'm sorry the office called you," I mumbled.

"They better have called me!" Mom picked dried glue off her fingertip. "The collages can wait."

Baby sighed and stretched out by the hearth.

"What about your cards?"

Mom patted my ankle. "Don't worry. I won't miss any deadlines. The cards will be ready to ship by Saturday."

Good. One less thing to worry about.

"Do you want to talk about what happened at school?"

I'd rather eat glass. "Not now."

"You sure?"

"I'm sure."

"Well, I was gluing the numbers on the clock when the school called…"

"Go," I said. "Time waits for no one."

"All right, if you're sure." Mom rose. "Shout if you need me."

I gave her my most reassuring smile. After she left, I moved to the hearth and snuggled Baby. She placed a warm, sympathetic paw on my leg. "Do you remember the last time we saw Dad?"

Baby lowered her head.

"Right." A sick feeling twisted my stomach. "Almost a year ago." Halloween. Parvani and I had decided to enter the costume contest at school. Dad had promised to take pictures of us, but at the last minute he had accepted an assignment. He'd come into my room while I'd been shoving my Dr. Jekyll lab coat into my backpack.

"Hey, Kitten. You weren't going to leave without saying goodbye, were you?" I could hear his voice as though it were yesterday.

"Goodbye." *Danger junkie.* I kept my chin down and yanked the zipper on my backpack. The metal teeth gnashed together, like stitches closing an angry wound.

"Mom's going to take a picture of you and Parvani in your costumes and email it to me." Dad held out the digital camera. "Why don't you take one of me before I leave?"

I slung my backpack over my shoulder. "Some other time, Dad. I gotta go. The carpool is waiting."

"Come on. Just one picture."

I scowled.

He held out his arms. "At least give me a farewell hug."

I relented and hugged him, breathing in his peppermint soap scent. He gave me a final squeeze, then swept his lucky hat off his head and put it on mine.

"Statistically speaking, Kitten, I'll be much safer in Afghanistan than I was in Iraq."

I glared at him from beneath the camouflage cap. "Whatever." My voice dripped sarcasm.

Dad frowned. "Evie…"

I banged the front door behind me.

Baby's nails dug into my leg, returning me to the present. I stared at the flames. I'd taken his hat, but not his picture. *Why? Why? I want a do-over.*

Guilt and regret consumed me. Chewed raw, I searched for a way to punish myself. Baby followed me into my room, then collapsed on the rag rug with a loud sigh. I pulled *Algebra for Dummies* out of my backpack. Not its real title, but it should have been.

Twenty problems. My misery index spiked.

I was on number sixteen, and pretty sure I had only gotten four correct, when the doorbell rang. Baby barked. My heart leapt out my chest and thudded into my beanbag chair. It couldn't be Parvani. She had piano today.

Mom never answers the door while she's working, so I trudged down the hall to investigate. "Salem?"

She rolled her heavily lined eyes. "Sarah," she corrected.

"Sorry. Come in."

She stepped into the entry and chewed her lipstick-covered lip. I recognized the color, Black Raspberry Glimmer, from an ad in *Kiss* and fought a twinge of envy.

"I have something for you." She swung around so I could see her backpack.

"Homework assignments?"

She sneered. "Hardly. Can we go to your room?"

The word "sure" left my mouth before I could stop it. I gestured toward the hall. "This way."

The hall is a gallery of sorts. The black and white, first-place winning shot I'd taken just before Dad died held a place of honor on the left wall. It showed a homeless woman I'd seen sitting on a bench near Well-Read Books. She had wrapped elastic bandages around her legs to ward off the cold, and wore a black garbage bag across her shoulders like a mink stole. She'd snuggled her dog, a moist-eyed Chihuahua, against her toothless, lined face.

I should have been proud of it, but looking at the photo set off a serious case of guilt and churned up painful memories. Mom had entered it in a photo contest. She'd been hoping if I won, I would get so stoked about photography that I'd start taking pictures again. Miss Roberts had seen the photo in the *Times*. When my predecessor had moved out of state, she'd remembered the photo and promoted me to editor for the yearbook.

I'm such a fraud.

But Jordan was worse than a fraud. After Dad's funeral, Jordan had tried to renew our friendship. So, like an idiot, I had invited him to go to the photo contest's award ceremony with me. I'd waited and waited. He hadn't showed. He hadn't even called.

"Evie," he'd told me the next day. "Man, I'm like, so sorry. I totally forgot about your gig. Bucky Lasek was at the Skate Shed signing autographs. Grandpa took me."

Like some skateboarding medalist was more important than my winning a national photo contest. Loser.

Fortunately, Dad's photographs from his stringer days in Asia and the Middle East had Salem engrossed. Parvani hated the one of the Taliban planting explosives in the Bamiyan Buddhas. Salem paused in front of it and frowned, but said nothing.

"Here's my room," I said, opening the door.

Salem lips curved into an amused smile when she spotted the Shay Stewart collage. "Nice shrine."

"Thanks."

Her gaze flickered over my math homework, then darted to the poop bag with the Quarter Guardians. The willow branch and Parvani's bag from Sage Mage were heaped beside it. Even more incriminating, the corner of *Teen Wytche* peeked out from beneath some soiled clothes.

"Hunter told me what happened today."

"Hunter?"

"The Goth in French class."

I sank onto my bed. "The 'Dude, take the picture' guy?"

Salem nodded and perched on the edge of my bed. "So I brought you some things." She pulled a blue plastic toiletry kit out of her backpack. "Close the door," she whispered.

I hesitated. Hadn't she heard of Red Ribbon Week and the whole "Do Not Do Drugs" speech? "Sarah, I don't…"

"They aren't *drugs*, moron."

"Oh. Sorry." I tiptoed to the door and closed it. The scratchy rip of the metal zipper and my own morbid curiosity lured me back to the bed.

Salem slid her hand under the lid and withdrew a large, silver pentacle. "It's an extra." She dropped it into my hand. "So you can have it."

The weight over my heart lifted a little. One more object I could check off the list. "Thanks, Sarah. I so appreciate it."

Her brow twitched. "There's more. You remember Amy?"

"Your perfect sister?"

"Well, she has a weakness for those free gifts you get sometimes when you buy makeup."

Who wouldn't?

Salem's features settled into a mask of mock pity. "Not all the shades of lipstick and eye shadow worked with her coloring. So Amy would dump the rejects into her bottom drawer." Salem pushed back the toiletry kit lid and revealed about ten tubes of lipstick and four eye shadow cases. "None of them have ever been used, so you don't have to worry about catching any dread diseases."

"Wow." My fingers flew to the forbidden tubes. Sparkle Dream. Nearly Nude. Dark Flame. *Mother lode.*

"I don't want to upset your mom. She looks like she's having a rough time. So you have to promise me something."

"Anything. What?"

"Promise you'll only use these when you need to throw a glamour."

"A what?"

"A glamour. An illusion." She glanced at the posters above my bed. "Like when Shay Stewart wore eyeliner and gold teeth in his pirate movie. He used makeup and costumes to create the illusion. They helped him *become* a pirate."

"So these are for Halloween?"

Salem shook her head. "Why do you think people call me Salem?"

"Because…" I bit off my words and took a long look at the black eyeliner spiraled toward her temples, her layers of medieval-inspired black clothing, and her skull and pentacle jewelry. "Because you're throwing a glamour?"

"Exactly."

"Why?"

"Because I was sick of every teacher telling me, 'You're Amy's little sister. I expect big things out of you.'"

"Now they don't make the connection?"

"Yep, and the pressure is off."

"Wow." I twirled a tube of Mad For Mauve lipstick between my fingers. "But I don't get it. What does any of this have to do with me?"

Salem released a long breath, then withdrew a recyclable grocery sack from her backpack. "You've lost your mojo." She laid wire-framed eyeglasses, a white crystal, and a plastic film canister on the bed.

I snatched up the black plastic container and popped its lid. *Empty.* "Where did you find this? Hardly anyone sells film these days."

"I found it in the glove compartment of Mom's car. It had probably been there for years," Salem explained. "About your mojo. To get it back, you need a talisman. Some item to make you feel like a photographer again."

I tried on the glasses. My vision blurred. "I don't know."

"I'm not asking you to dress like Annie Leibovitz or Imogene Cunningham. Just find a secret object. What would give you courage?"

"I'm not sure courage can be found in a tube of Positively Pink lip gloss."

"Maybe not." Salem rose and shrugged into her empty backpack. "But you'll know the right thing when you see it." She slipped off the bed. "I better go. Einstein shreds tissue boxes if he isn't fed by four."

I walked her to the front door. "Thanks, Sarah."

"You're welcome. Good luck." She clutched her black spider web poncho closer to her wraith-like body and headed into the swirl of leaves and wind.

I closed the door behind her. First a spell, and now a glamour and a talisman? This was more confusing than algebra.

But what if I could carry it off?

CHAPTER NINE

"Why are you wearing a film canister around your neck?" Parvani asked during carpool the next morning.

Her twin brothers started arguing over whose turn it was to use the latest, must-have electronic device, saving me from answering. As chaos shook the back seat, I hunched in the front and tucked the makeshift necklace under my Cal sweatshirt. It made an awkward bulge, like I wore an inhaler or something. While Dr. Hyde-Smith threatened to pull over if the Terrors didn't knock it off, I slipped the canister into my backpack next to one of the forbidden tubes of lipstick.

Some talisman. I didn't feel empowered. I felt like an idiot.

Dr. Hyde-Smith glided the Lexus up to the school's back entrance. Parvani and I jumped out and shut the door on the twins' battle. A fine mist settled over us as we slipped through the cyclone gate.

Parvani nudged me. "Look."

Jordan walked several yards ahead, his shoulders back, as if his backpack weighed little more than a dragonfly. With each step his sneakers sunk a little into the saturated turf and made a small sucking sound. I wondered if a camera could capture the mist sparkling on his hair.

"I love the way everything is so effortless with him," Parvani said in a dreamy voice. "Let's go ahead with the spell."

Arrow to the heart. I forced myself to look away from Jordan. "I don't think so..."

"Come on. You promised."

"No, I didn't. But I did find the Quarter Guardians and Salem gave me a pentacle."

Parvani seized my arm. "She did?"

"Ow. Yes. And Baby may have found a wand. Now all you need are Goddess and God figures."

The bell rang. Dr. Hyde-Smith had made us late again. At least when Mom drove, we got to school on time. Parvani and I broke into a run, which wasn't easy carrying thirty pounds of books on my back. Fixing my gaze on Jordan, I wondered how he made sprinting look so easy.

I arrived at English sweaty and no doubt red-faced. Salem threw me a searching look. I shrugged. I wasn't sure if my make-shift talisman would work, even with the milky crystal rattling inside it.

Five short periods separated me from Yearbook. I'd find out then.

Mrs. Knapp handed back our vocabulary tests. Salem's had a scarlet C- scrawled across the top. She flipped it upside down, then flicked her head as if to prove she didn't care.

I received an A with a smiley face drawn beside it. A warm, happy feeling curled around me, like one of Parvani's cashmere scarves. The happiness lasted fifty minutes —until Gym.

Coach Willis divided us into two teams for Capture the Flag. Parvani got stuck with Evan and Tommy. At least she didn't have to worry about them holding her prisoner. I slipped my hand into my jeans pocket and clutched the topaz. *Please don't let me run the wrong way or be captured by the Smash Heads.*

Someone nudged my shoulder, and I inhaled the improbable yet wonderful dry-weed scent of an Indian summer. "Hey, Evie."

I pulled my hand out of my pocket. "Hey, Jordan."

"About yesterday —"

A couple of boys jostled us from behind. Jordan flashed them a look. When he glanced back at me, his expression softened. "We're on the same team." He said it as though he meant something deeper, something more than just this game.

My mind flashed back to a photo Dad had taken the summer Jordan and I had been four. Our families had gone to Disneyland together. Jordan and I had both wanted to pull Excalibur, King Arthur's sword, from the stone. Jordan had reached the top of the rock first, but had been unable to budge the gilded weapon.

"Come on, Evie, you try."

So I had climbed up in my pink flowered dress, my strawberry hair sticking out from my pink striped baseball cap, and pulled.

Nothing.

Jordan had wiped his hands on his rugby shirt, then held up three fingers. "On the count of three." We'd sat on either side of the sword, and at the moment we'd grasped the gold hilt, Dad had snapped the picture.

Coach's shrill whistle jolted me back to the present. Jordan nodded toward the Smash Heads. "Let's get them."

The game was in play.

A few students were shoved like human sacrifices across the dividing border. Jordan paced the front line. Since I didn't want to be abandoned to the pack, I shadowed him. A mischievous expression lit his face. "Suicide mission?"

"Sure." *No! Are you crazy? Why tempt fate? Gym is already close enough to death.*

An image of Dad flashed into my mind. How could I joke about death? Guilt knotted my stomach like three-day-old fish. I wondered if Jordan would catch me if I fainted. Probably, but then Parvani would kill me.

I took a deep breath. If — okay, *when* I got captured—at least Parvani would visit me in jail. Unless the Smash Heads got to me first.

"You don't have to if you don't want to," Jordan said.

I glanced at Tommy and Evan, who were disobeying the code of conduct by pummeling rather than tagging. Where the heck was Coach?

Jordan whispered, "On the count of three, okay? One…"

My heart beat too fast.

"Two…"

I couldn't draw oxygen into my lungs.

"Three!"

We bolted like twin roller coasters. I ran faster than I ever thought possible. Smoke probably hissed from my sneakers. The Smash Heads, sensing fresh blood, pivoted toward me. Even though Parvani was on their team, she chased after them. Tommy, a towering year older because he had been held back in the third grade, barreled toward me.

I froze.

"Evie, keep moving!" Jordan yelled.

Before I could take a step, Parvani overtook the Smash Heads and cut in front of them. Tommy pushed her out of the way. Judging from the determined expression on his face, I was next.

Jordan threw himself at the Smash Heads. The three tackled each other with an awful crunching sound.

Behind me, my team screamed, "Evie, *run!*"

I sprinted as though the demons of the underworld were at my heels. Ahead, the orange team's flag rippled in the breeze from atop its four-foot pole. To my right, five of my team members yelled from the jail zone. Knowing I'd need their help, I zigzagged.

"Jail break!" I stormed the jail, affecting their release. Joyous screams filled the autumn air.

The whistle shrilled. Coach Willis strode onto the field, where Tommy and Evan clung to Jordan like vile leeches.

"Jordan! Tommy! Evan! Unnecessary roughness. Everyone in the class, run a lap."

Several students booed. I could have sworn Jordan winked at me. My stomach fluttered. I leaned over, hands clutching my thighs, and dragged air into my lungs.

Parvani caught up with me. "Are you okay?"

I nodded. The pack swept us up into a slow jog.

"Can you believe he defended my honor?" Parvani knocked a clump of muddy grass from her jeans.

"Who? Jordan?"

She scrunched up her face. "Of course Jordan."

Funny, I could have sworn he'd taken down the Smash Heads to protect *me*. Not wanting to argue, I changed the subject. "You were awesome. I can't believe you cut in front of Tommy."

"I'm glad my team didn't boo me. And you! I couldn't believe your suicide run. What possessed you?"

Jordan.

I shrugged and acted like I was too out of breath to talk. When Parvani wasn't looking, I searched the ragtag runners for a head of highlighted wavy brown hair. I spotted him just as he glanced back. Our gaze collided and his smile made me falter and almost fall.

I had entered Jordanland, and I didn't know how to turn back.

CHAPTER TEN

"Evie, may I see you?" Señora Allende asked as the bell rang and students hurried off to lunch.

If my math teacher had uttered those words, I'd be dry heaving. But since Spanish is one of my best subjects, I said, "Sure." I shouldered my backpack and waited for the room to clear before approaching Señora's cluttered desk.

"A unique situation has arisen." Señora brushed back her salt-and-pepper hair. It was cut along her jawline, framing her high cheekbones. "I have an excellent student," she continued, "who anticipates missing class a lot over the next month."

"Is she sick?" My mind flashed back to a girl who had become anorexic last year and had to be hospitalized for six weeks.

"No, he isn't sick. But he does want the nature of his absences to be kept secret. He's an A student, and doesn't want to fall behind. He's only available for tutoring on Saturdays at four o'clock."

I shifted my weight, putting two and two together and actually reaching four. "So he can't go to the Tutoring Center."

"No, and I'm unavailable on Saturdays due to a family commitment." Señora jabbed a well-chewed pencil into the crowded mesh cup on her desk. "Which is where you come in.

The boy is a fellow freshman. He wants someone trustworthy to help him keep up. You would earn ten dollars an hour."

A vision of Alexander Hamilton greenbacks leapfrogged in my mind. There were two boys in the school I would refuse to help, and one of them took French. I prayed the other took German. "It isn't Tommy Deitch, is it?"

Señora snorted. Tommy's name must have come up a few times in the teacher's lounge. "No, it's not Tommy."

"Then I'll do it."

"*¡Bueno!* He can meet you at your house or the library, whichever is more convenient for you."

A pang of worry knotted my stomach. I didn't want some mansion *muchacho* making fun of our cracked tile and running toilet. The library would be a better meeting place, but then my mom would have to drive me.

Señora pulled her purse out of her desk drawer then stood. "He'll need to start this weekend."

I decided to risk it. "Okay, tell him my house."

Señora beamed. "*Muchas gracias,* Evie. I'll give Zhù your address."

Confusion skidded across my brain. "Zhù Wong?"

"*Sí.* You know him?"

"He's a friend of a friend." I wondered what would make Zhù miss class. Maybe she hadn't told me the truth. Maybe he was ill.

Señora dragged her purse strap over her shoulder. "Please respect his privacy and tell no one."

I hoped Zhù didn't have something life-threatening. Parvani would never forgive me for keeping it from her. "I promise not to tell."

"*Bueno.*"

Dismissed, I headed out the door and down the hall, no doubt frowning just like Mom. A few students had clustered under the overhang near the lockers, but everyone else seemed to be in the cafeteria already. I rounded the corner of the building and almost ran into Miss Ravenwood.

The temperature plummeted at least ten degrees. Miss Ravenwood scowled down at me and I swear I heard the witch's theme song from *The Wizard of Oz*. I clutched my Spanish folder to my chest and averted my gaze. Miss Ravenwood swept past me, her disdain palpable.

I blew out a long breath. For once, I was glad I sucked at math.

Parvani and, to my surprise, Salem, were waiting for me outside Mr. Ross's door.

"Where have you been?" Parvani asked.

"Señora Allende needed to ask..."

Mr. Ross poked his head out. "Girls? I have to take off. If you want to use the room you'll have to come in now and lock the door."

"May Sarah join us?" Parvani pushed her glasses higher up her nose. "We promise we won't let anyone else in."

Mr. Ross hesitated. His glance flicked over Salem's eyebrow stud and makeup. Instead of her usual neo-medieval blouse, she wore a black tee shirt emblazoned with a skull and crossbones. He probably wondered how many school supplies she would steal. I held my breath, willing him to trust our judgment.

"Okay, she can stay," he finally said. "But no one else." We let ourselves in while he checked his pockets for his keys. "I'll be back soon," he warned. The heavy door closed behind him with a click.

We threw our backpacks on the table nearest the television and scraped back three molded plastic chairs. "I was going through my parents' old yearbooks last night," Salem said in a conspiratorial whisper. "And I found this." She pulled a mud-colored yearbook out of her pack. *Jefferson High School, 1974* angled in pale green lettering across the front.

"My parents were eleventh graders in '74." Salem opened the yearbook to a page she had marked with a hot pink sticky note. "But look at the ninth grade class." She pointed to a flinty-eyed girl on the right hand page.

"Miss Ravenwood?" Parvani said in disbelief. "She went *here?*"

My parents had graduated from Jefferson, too. I did some quick subtraction on my fingers. "Wait a minute." I glanced at the names accompanying the photos on the left hand page, and there it was, like a sucker punch, *Deaman O'Reilly.* Dad, fourteen years old, his hair windblown and his eyes bright with imagined adventure.

"Did you find it?" Salem asked.

"Yes." The word came out as a croak.

Parvani leaned closer to the page. "What?"

"Evie's mom. Her picture is here too."

"My mother?" I scanned the rows of smiling faces. Mom's familiar, knowing eyes snagged my attention. *Olivia Portland.*

"Am I right?" Salem asked.

"Yes." I drifted back to Dad.

Parvani gasped and pointed to his picture. "There's Evie's father."

Salem bent over the page. "But his byline always says Dash O'Reilly."

"Said," I corrected, my voice thick. "A fellow cameraman gave him the nickname because he was always dashing into danger."

The laugh track erupted on the television.

"I bet they knew each other," Parvani said. "Evie, you should ask your mom."

"I will."

"Maybe you could find her yearbook," Parvani suggested. "See if Miss Ravenwood wrote anything in it."

Bad blood. No wonder Mom had stiffened when she saw Miss Ravenwood in Sage Mage.

Parvani clapped her hands together. "Maybe Miss Ravenwood put a curse on you when you were born. It would explain why you can't do math."

"Right." Salem rolled her eyes.

My gaze darted from Dad, to Mom, to Miss Ravenwood. The musty yearbook smell had faded, driven away by a spicy, gypsy scent. I glanced at the door, certain I heard the distant tinkle of tiny pewter bells.

CHAPTER ELEVEN

I slunk into Algebra, the self-esteem sucking black hole, and took my seat. Mr. Bentley was scribbling on the blackboard. His military-style buzz cut glistened beneath the fluorescent lights, and the pockets of his navy slacks were streaked with chalk.

My stomach growled. In all the commotion, I had skipped lunch. Great. Now I'd be even less able to concentrate than usual. As I pulled out my homework, I wondered if Miss Ravenwood really *had* cursed me.

Mr. Bentley wrote:

Hardy-Weinberg Equilibrium
p=the frequency of the dominant allele A
q=the frequency of the recessive allele a
The sum of the alleles must = 100%

Mr. Bentley might as well have said, "Two trains left the station at the same time. If Train A was going x miles an hour and Train B was going…" *Kill me now.*

The person in front of me handed back copies of a blank graph. I placed one of the graphs on top of my notebook and passed the remaining sheets to the stoner behind me. Chalk screeched against the blackboard. From beneath the sweat-stained brim of Dad's cap, I watched Mr. Bentley write: *p2 + 2pq = q2 + 1.*

The little squares on the graph blurred. I planted my elbows on the desk and clutched the sides of my head. Old resentment spiraled through me. *I bet Jordan already knows all this. Parvani too.*

The second hand on the wall clock ticked. Twelve-fifty and one second, twelve-fifty and two seconds, twelve-fifty and three seconds…

"Quiz on Friday, ladies and gentlemen."

A sinking, nauseous feeling slammed my insides. *I hope* Teen Wytche *has a spell for improving your math grade.*

***

I needed a boost to face Yearbook. I needed to feel like someone other than Evie O'Reilly, loser. So I ducked into the girls' bathroom. Guilt and excitement warred within me as I fished the tube of Nearly Nude lipstick out of my backpack. I'd once heard an anchorwoman on television say you should wear lipstick the same color as your tongue. Weird, I know, but the reds fought with my Intensely Autumn hair. The bronzes made me look ill. No way could I show up wearing one of Salem's black-death shades.

The Nearly Nude lipstick had a faint petroleum smell and tasted a little yucky. Still, I could almost be mistaken for hot. Mom would so ground me for a month.

I'll let Jordan see me in Biology, I decided, *and then wipe / off the lipstick before I cross the field.* Mom would never know.

I slipped the film can necklace over my head for added confidence, and prayed I wouldn't run into either of the Smash Heads. Hallie, my formerly ill photographer, strode up the ramp to Room

222. Relieved, I nearly kissed the plastic necklace. Maybe I *had* found my talisman.

"We have lots of work to do today," Miss Roberts announced as I took my seat. "I'd like to meet with the layout artists to discuss concept ideas. Photographers..." She eyed the room. "I see Zhù isn't here today. Hallie, grab a camera. We need more fashion photos. Evie..."

The wall phone rang. While Miss Roberts walked over to it, I glanced toward the door and willed Zhù to materialize.

Miss Roberts hung up the phone and sighed. "Evie, you are wanted in the office."

The lipstick burned my lips. *Mom knows.* Had the school installed a spy camera in the bathroom? *I am so dead.* Then my heart splashed down somewhere in my large intestine. I've been called to the office once before — the day my dad had died.

I grabbed my backpack. Heat flooded my neck and face — I was sure all eyes were on me. At least Jordan wasn't in this class. Miss Roberts said something about caption writers. A hum like a funeral dirge swelled in my ears, drowning her words.

Outside, I pulled a tissue from the front pocket of my back-pack and swiped at my lips while I walked the empty corridor between the two hundred and three hundred blocks of classrooms. The office was just beyond the bathrooms, across from Room 301 and a cluster of lockers. I swallowed hard and opened the door.

I half hoped and half dreaded Mom would be there. She wasn't. If she didn't know about the lipstick, then something must have happened to her or Nana...

"Evie?"

I flinched, heart in turbo-panic. "Yes?"

Mrs. Scroggins, the school secretary, stared down her bifocals. "Miss Gaya would like a word with you."

"Miss Gaya?"

"The new counselor." Mrs. Scroggins led me down the Employees Only hall to a back office. The door stood ajar. An air of counting-the-years-to-retirement clung to the middle-aged woman seated behind the metal desk. Seeing me, she rose from her chair.

"Thank you, Mrs. Scroggins." Miss Gaya's layered, filmy green dress swayed as she leaned across the desk and shook my hand. "You must be Evie O'Reilly."

"Yes, I am. Is my mother all right?"

"Please be seated. Your mother is fine. I just called her."

I sank into the blue plastic chair.

Miss Gaya closed the door then returned to her seat. Her gaze jumped to my film can necklace then back up to my eyes.

"I understand you weren't well in Yearbook yesterday. How are you feeling today?"

I forced a smile. "Well, thank you."

"Good." Miss Gaya pushed up her sleeves and gave me a long look. I got the distinct feeling she didn't believe me. I shifted in my seat and wished the old school counselor wasn't on maternity leave.

"Your friends are worried about you, Evie. So I wanted to introduce myself and see if I can help you in any way."

Yeah, like you'd know anything about solving my problems.

Miss Gaya clasped her hands together and hunched forward. "Is there anything you'd like to talk about?"

Several things flashed through my mind — the love spell, Jordan and Parvani, Dad, Mom, and Miss Ravenwood, getting out of Biology, and again, the love spell.

"No," I said.

She nodded and leaned back in her chair. The small office grew quiet. My stomach growled. Out in the hall, the copy machine hummed to life. Miss Gaya picked up a pen and held it between her fingers like a cigarette. "It's been almost a year since your father died?"

A lump rose in my throat. "Yes."

"It must be difficult for you and your mother."

"We're managing." *Sort of.* "Mom joined a widows' support group."

"Excellent. And are you still seeing a grief counselor?"

"Nah." *Do you have any idea how much therapy costs? How much groceries and gas cost?* "Mom wanted me to keep going, but I told her I was fine."

Miss Gaya tapped her pen against a folder on her desk. I got the feeling she believed me about as much as Mom had. "You have a strong circle of friends, Evie. They'll help you if you let them. And I'm here too if you ever need me."

What circle of friends? I wondered. Who besides Parvani? I stumbled to my feet. "Thank you, Miss Gaya. I should get back to Yearbook. Our first deadline is in eight days."

"Of course. Remember, my door is always open."

I swiveled and faced the closed door. *Right.*

When I returned to class, Miss Roberts was shoulder-deep in noisy layout artists. I tiptoed over to the computer and booted up the program for working with digital photos. Surely by now, Zhù had arrived and was off taking pictures. *Unless he does have a dread disease.*

I glanced up at the wall clock. If I kept low for fifteen more minutes, then I could escape to Biology and sit behind Jordan and daydream.

CHAPTER TWELVE

Jordan's hair kind of waved in the back. The ends curled, just skimming his shoulder. I wondered what he'd do if I reached out and wrapped one of the curls around my finger…

"Miss O'Reilly!"

I snapped my gaze from the back of Jordan's head to the front of the classroom. Mr. Esenberg glared at me, a stub of white chalk clutched between his thumb and forefinger. He was well over six feet tall and as wiry as a chenille pipe cleaner.

I sat up straighter, heat flooding my neck. "Yes, sir?"

"Switch seats with Mr. Kent, please."

My heart bungee-jumped to my feet. I closed my biology notebook, horrified to find I had doodled hearts around the binder ring holes. A jock two rows over laughed and said, "What did you do now, Kent?"

Jordan kept his mouth shut, closed his biology book, and whisked it up with his notebook.

I reached down for my backpack. The pencil I had stuck above my ear and forgotten about clattered onto the scuffed linoleum. It rolled under Jordan's chair. He retrieved it, rose, and with his back to Mr. Esenberg, winked as he handed it to me.

"Sorry," I mouthed. I slid into Jordan's seat, quaking under Mr. Esenberg's watchful eyes. Jordan's body heat still clung to the wood. A fresh blush flamed toward my eyebrows as his warmth seeped through my jeans. I heard the soft thud of Jordan's textbook landing on the desk behind me. My former chair creaked, and then I heard Jordan's sneaker-shod feet slide toward me.

"Perhaps you can see the board better now, Miss O'Reilly." Mr. Esenberg *almost* kept the snarkiness out of his voice.

I nodded, afraid to speak. The doomed feeling I get in math class oozed into me. I slumped low in my chair and glanced at the clock. Twenty-five minutes left. No way would I make it. My scalp prickled. I sensed Jordan's stare and regretted not getting up early enough to wash my hair.

Mr. Esenberg wrote on the chalkboard. *Independent and Dependent Variables.* It sounded like math. I tapped my pencil against my desk.

Mr. Esenberg spun around and glared. My pencil stilled. Trapped in the second row, I caught a faint whiff of the salami Mr. Esenberg must have eaten for lunch.

Somewhere off to the right, a cell phone beeped.

"When we are given an equation for exponential population growth, there are several variables," Mr. Esenberg explained. "We must distinguish between them in order to interpret the equation and graph it. Miss O'Reilly, given this equation," he wrote $G = rN$ on the board, "where G represents the growth of a population, N is the initial population size, and r is the intrinsic rate of increase, what do you predict the growth of the population will be when the intrinsic rate of increase is a large number as opposed to a smaller number?"

My heart jackhammered and my eyes felt like overheated flashbulbs. Mind blank, I cleared my throat. "The population will increase more," I ventured in a decibel barely audible to humans.

"Ah. Class, please take a moment to write down your own predictions. Then we shall see if Miss O'Reilly's extrapolation is correct."

The sounds of twenty-five pencils scratching across notebook paper filled the room, punctuated by the slow tick of the wall clock.

"Well, class. I believe we have identified the correct answer. Can anyone guess what the definition of an independent and dependent variable is, and identify them in this equation?"

My heart galloped. I thought a moment, then wrote in my notebook.

"Miss O'Reilly. Since you seem to be on a roll today, please read your prediction to the class."

His voice sounded neutral, but I sensed a trap. The room grew so quiet I could hear the ends of my hair split. "The r is independent, and the G is dependent?"

"Ah." Mr. Esenberg's tall, wiry frame bent into a question mark. "Would you mind telling us why?"

"Because depending on how we define r, G changes?" I ventured.

The desk behind me squeaked. "Way to go," Jordan whispered.

I exhaled. I glowed. Relief and happiness radiated from my every pore.

Then Mr. Esenberg started talking about graphing our observations on an X-Y plane. Surely my fresh waves of despair were obvious to the entire class. Those aware of my math disability could predict I would now flunk Biology as well as math. *Jordan knows.*

Mr. Esenberg dragged a flip chart from the corner of the room to a spot near the table. "We have lots of experiments coming up, class, so you'll each work with a partner." Squeals and moans bounced between the students. Mr. Esenberg flipped back the top sheet. "Read them and weep."

I scanned the list. For the most part, Mr. Esenberg had assigned pairs according to the alphabet. Realization tiptoed down the back of my neck. There it was in bold blue sharpie: Kent/O'Reilly.

My heart toggled between excitement and hope, and then freefell into dread. *Today was a fluke. I lucked out with my answers. But Jordan knows I can't do this stuff. He'd never want to work with me.* The bell rang, jerking me from my seat. I shoved my science stuff into my backpack and rushed out the door. *No way will I stick around while he asks for a better lab partner.*

As I shouldered my way into the crowd heading for the football field, I prayed Parvani's mom would be on time for once and waiting for us in the carpool lane.

CHAPTER THIRTEEN

By the time Mrs. Hyde-Smith drove up to the curb, the parking lot had emptied, the yellow schools buses had long since lurched off, and the football field was deserted. I could have spent all that time in the office trying to talk the registrar into switching me out of Biology. I glanced down at Parvani's watch. School had ended twenty minutes ago. Mom must be ballistic by now.

"Gee, Mother. Thanks for showing up." Parvani hurled her backpack on the floor of the Jag, then scooted across the leather seat. She stabbed her seatbelt buckle into its receptacle like she was loading a gun. Terribly un-Zen.

"Sorry. I was running errands." Mrs. Hyde-Smith checked her flawless lipstick in the rearview mirror.

Parvani crossed her arms over her chest. I knew she was imagining how many Nordstrom bags were hidden in the trunk. I wondered where the Terrors were — maybe locked up next to the shopping bags.

Mom opened the door as we purred into the driveway. "Sorry!" Mrs. Hyde-Smith called out through the rolled-down window. Mom dismissed her with a curt wave.

"You're not in your studio," I said as she closed the door behind us.

"I'm ironing." I could tell by her tone she'd been worried. "Would you like a snack?" Mom asked.

"No thanks. I'll just get my homework out of the way."

Mom shot me her when-did-aliens-take-over-your-mind look. I pretended not to notice and headed for my room. My heart beat way too fast, as if I had chugged caffeinated soda on an empty stomach.

"I seriously need help with Algebra and Biology," I told Baby as she followed me into my room. I knelt by the green beanbag chair and picked up *Teen Wytche*. Maybe it contained a spell, or talisman, or *something* to keep me from flunking.

Goosebumps sprouted on my arms as I opened the cover. The pages were no longer paper. The text was no longer machine printed. The words flowed in a spidery scrawl across ancient vellum. Ink smudged the goatskin, or whatever it was, as if the writer had hurried to get her thoughts down.

I dropped the book and threw the beanbag chair on top of it. For a second, I only heard the thudding of my heart. Then the beans in the beanbag started to rattle. I backed up and grabbed a huge stuffed rabbit and hugged it to my chest, peeking over its long, floppy ears.

Something fluttered in my peripheral vision. A Shay Stewart photo floated to the floor. Then another one detached from the wall and freefell.

The beans stopped rattling. A sudden chill enveloped the room. The windows were closed — no breeze. The fine hairs on my arm stood on end. In a fit of madness or misguided courage, I placed the bunny on the floor and lifted the beanbag chair.

The grimoire had grown to the size of a photo album. It flew open, and the pages riffled as though stirred by a strong wind. I dropped the beanbag on the rag rug, grabbed a chocolate-stained skirt from the floor, and hid my face behind it.

So much for courage.

My nose twitched at the faint incense smell rising from the grimoire. A framed photo of Parvani and me, taken from arm's length with my old 35mm camera, dove off my desk and thudded onto a pile of dirty jeans.

"Stop that!" I threw down the skirt. I gave my desk and the Shay Stewart shrine a quick glance. No more jumpers. Narrowing my eyes to slits, I glanced down. The book had fallen open to a page marked *Correspondences.* The word *wisdom* leaped out at me. My fingertip rasped against the paper as I skimmed across the list. Yellow. Sage. Sunflower.

A wisdom spell? It involved something about days of the week and planetary hours. The latter involved math, so I ignored it, hoping it wasn't too important. I rose to my feet and jogged down the hall. Baby scurried behind me, her toenails clicking across the tile in the entry.

A few minutes later, I dumped an armful of items on the rag rug, then shooed Baby into the hall. She whimpered as I locked my bedroom door.

After rooting through my desk drawer, I produced the compass Dad had given me back when I'd been a Girl Scout. The red needle wobbled toward north. I dragged out the river rocks and placed them at each compass point. "Okay, Quarter Guardians." Parvani must have highlighted a paragraph or two about them. I should have looked it up, but decided I didn't have time. Mom could appear at any moment to check on me.

The river rocks established the parameters for my invisible circle. In the center, I placed a yellow plate with an orange poppy design. Squatting, I slathered slippery sunflower oil onto a birthday candle. Once coated, the yellow candle glistened. I sprinkled it with sage from the spice drawer. The effect wasn't pretty, but then neither are math or science. Since the candle was too small for a candleholder, I pressed a glob of silly putty onto the plate and impaled it with the candle.

What else had been on Parvani's list? The pentacle. After wiping my oil-slick hands on a tissue, I dug out Salem's necklace and put it on. We hadn't found god and goddess figures yet, so I plucked a rainbow haired troll doll from my wicker hutch and placed it next to the plate. A dusty rhinestone tiara from a long-ago princess party sat in for the goddess.

I wrote the words *math, science, graphs,* and *Hardy-Weinberg* on a piece of binder paper along with *help* and *good grades.* Praying I wouldn't set off the smoke detector — or worse, burn down the house — I struck a wooden kitchen match, recoiling a bit when the sulfur burned a path up my nose. The candlewick flared. I blew out the match, almost extinguishing the candle as well, which probably would have jinxed the whole thing.

Weren't spells supposed to rhyme? If so, I was hosed, because I doubted anything would rhyme with Weinberg or science. Finally, figuring spells were just prayers with props, I sat down on the rag rug and prayed for wisdom. And clarity. And help. And to not look stupid in front of Jordan. Then, not wanting to appear greedy, I added, *Please just help me through Friday so I can pass the algebra quiz.*

Behind me, the doorknob rattled. "Evie? Why is your door locked?"

"Just a sec, Mom." I licked my fingers and extinguished the candle.

I cracked open the door. "Yes?"

Mom's nose crinkled. "Have you been lighting matches?"

Unable to come up with a plausible lie, I resorted to the truth. "I lit a candle."

Mom sniffed again. The lines that had become embedded in her forehead since Dad's death grew deeper.

"I'm trying to study," I reminded her.

"All right." She drew out the words as if weighing whether to believe me. "How does pasta at six-thirty sound?"

"Fine."

Mom narrowed her eyes. For a second I feared she'd push the door open. She didn't. Maybe the Quarter Guardians had kept her out. "Later, alligator." Mom headed for the studio she and Dad had built over the garage.

I glanced back at my circle. The rainbow-haired troll appeared amused. *Maybe because of the candle stuck in the silly putty.* Then I noticed Jordan's photo, the one I had hidden among the belts, had fallen off the shelf again and landed face up in the circle next to the candle.

My jaw dropped. "No," I told the grimoire. "This can't be. Stop throwing us together."

I heard a soft puff of air, as if someone were blowing bubbles through a wand. Pink vapor rose from the open spell book, and the scent of summer roses perfumed the room.

"You didn't say anything about roses and wisdom."

I could have sworn the book uttered an exasperated sigh before it slammed shut.

My heart constricted. I gave Jordan's photo one last look before I hid it under my mattress. The troll doll beamed wide-eyed approval as I shoved the Quarter Guardians back into Baby's unused poop bag. "Stop looking so happy," I warned the troll.

Realizing I sounded crazy, I shoved *Teen Wytche* under a pile of dirty clothes and headed to the bathroom for a hot, cleansing shower.

CHAPTER FOURTEEN

The doorbell, which Nana had installed during one of her wry moments, sent the opening bars of the "Mission Impossible" theme thundering through the house. Baby lumbered to her feet, barking, and bounded down the hall.

"Mom! Can you get it?" I unwrapped the bath towel from around my wet hair and listened. No screeching stove fan. No simmering garlic-and-shallot smell wafting down the hall. Mom must still be in her studio.

The bell rang again. It had to be Salem. Parvani would have called.

The barking stopped, and I heard Baby skid across the entry tile. I threw the damp towel on the rag rug, just outside the magic circle. I pulled on my plaid flannel pants in a rush, facing them inside out so the huge Cal logo wouldn't draw too much attention to my butt. Water dripped down my back, chilling my bare flesh. I whipped the pentacle necklace over my head, then hurried into a pink satin bra and a cleanish yellow hoodie. I stashed the candle inside my jewelry box, then, having no idea where I'd left my shoes, slid on some frayed slippers and headed down the hall.

As I rounded the corner, I noticed a figure pressed against one of the narrow windows flanking the door. Jordan! Heat rushed up my throat. Every cell screamed *run,* but he had already seen me and waved.

I opened the door, my breath rattling like tumbleweeds inside my chest. "Jordan."

"Hey, Evie." He gave me a once over. "I like the wet hair look. Nice slippers. Though I kinda preferred your pink bunnies."

My brain felt microwaved. "The ones I wore when we were six?"

Light danced in Jordan's eyes. "Yeah." He bent and petted Baby. "Did you eat the bunnies, Baby Girl?"

Baby wagged her tail.

"So, can I come in?"

The kitchen door slammed. Mom must have come down to make dinner.

"Um, sure."

Jordan stepped inside and hesitated, raking his fingers through his highlights. When we were younger, he would have run down the hall to my room. Mortification crept over me as I thought of Jordan seeing my Shay Stewart shrine, the magic circle, and my unmade bed. I gestured toward the living room.

This part of the house is so not Mom's or my style. Dad's parents had given us the black leather sofa and chair three years ago, right before they'd moved to Bangkok. Mom had tried to soften the starkness by adding a scuffed wooden coffee table and white tea light candles. I guess it helped a little. Enlarged prints of Dad's photos adorned the wine-colored wall behind the sofa. Dad had clustered my photo series on homeless people and their pets on the end wall, above the chair.

Jordan plopped down on the white shag carpet, leaned against the couch, and unfolded his legs beneath the low table. He jiggled his foot, a sure sign he was nervous.

I perched on the chair, plotting my escape, certain he was about to dump me for a lab partner who understood an x/y axis and Hardy-Weinberg. Jordan patted the floor beside him and gave me one of his puppy dog looks. If Parvani had been here, she would have squealed.

"What's up?" I tried to sound nonchalant as I lowered myself onto the carpet. Baby wormed between us and rested her head on Jordan's thigh, drooling on his jeans.

"See, she remembers me." Jordan pushed up the sleeves of his rugby shirt, exposing skin still golden-brown from skateboard camp. He propped his elbow on the sofa. His nearness charged the air between us. The fine hairs on my forearm stood on end. "You ran out of Biology pretty fast. Are you mad at me?"

I blinked several times as my mind processed. He'd noticed I had left in a hurry?

"I'm sorry I ratted you out to Miss Gaya," Jordan said in a rush.

"*You* talked to the school counselor about me?"

"I thought you knew." He reached over and fingered my hair, like he used to do when we were kids. His hand smelled of sunshine and pines and freshly mown grass. I struggled to concentrate. A startled look jumped into Jordan's eyes, as though he'd just realized we weren't five anymore. He withdrew his hand. Suddenly, I wanted to swallow my pride and ask Mom to take me to her hairdresser so I could get my old color back.

Get my old life back.

"Why did you go to Miss Gaya?"

"You know." Jordan's voice cracked and he stopped to clear his throat. "First your dad died. Then you went all, like, Halloween with your hair."

"*You* got highlights."

"Because Evan dared me. He said he'd donate thirty dollars to the VFW if I did."

"VFW?"

"Veterans of Foreign Wars. Grandpa belongs to it. I guess Evan's older brother does too, since he served in Iraq."

"Oh."

"And then yesterday," Jordan continued, "Parvani had to take you to the nurse. I felt, like, maybe you needed some help." He shrugged as his voice trailed off.

Stunned, I tried to decide whether to be furious or touched.

"So, are you mad at me?" He lowered his arm, and his fingers grazed my back, zapping a tingle to my core.

The phone rang. The sound registered in the back of my mind. "I'm not mad because you went to Miss Gaya," I decided aloud. *Ditching me for Bucky and the Smash Heads, yes.*

Jordan blew a long breath out his nose. "Good, 'cause…"

"Parvani called," Mom said as she entered the room in a garlic-scented cloud. Seeing Jordan, her eyes widened.

My heart flat-lined. *Parvani. The spell.*

Mom wiped her hands on her green *Kiss the Cook* apron. "Jordan, how nice to see you again. Would you like to stay for dinner? We're having pasta."

Jordan extricated his long legs from under the coffee table. "Thanks Mrs. O, but I can't. Mom has a committee meeting tonight and Dad has to prepare for a trial, so I need to hang with Grandpa."

"How is he doing?" I asked.

Jordan shrugged like everything was fine, but we both knew it wasn't. "He's… having memory issues."

Mom placed her hand on Jordan's shoulder. "I'm sorry. I know it's tough." She glanced at me. "Evie, I thought you were doing homework, so I told Parvani you'd call her back."

I nodded, determined to tell Parvani I resigned from helping her with the love spell. Mom headed back to the kitchen. I walked Jordan to the entry and opened the door. "Thanks for looking out for me."

"You're welcome." He leaned over, and for a heart-stopping moment I thought he might kiss me. "Chill," he whispered, his breath a warm caress upon my ear.

My heart yo-yoed. "Not in my vocabulary, Clark."

His lips softened. "Can't remember the last time you called me Clark. Guess now you're, like, Lois Lane." He used to call me "Jimmy" after the red-haired photographer in the Superman comics. Apparently I didn't qualify anymore.

I pushed Jordan away. Bitterness crept into my voice. "Lois probably understood math."

He angled his head in a cute puppy sort of way. "Doubt it. Look how long it took her to figure out Superman's true identity."

With an athlete's easy grace, he picked up his helmet from the bench outside the door and put it on. Once he'd secured the strap, he retrieved his skateboard, which he'd propped against a flowerpot bursting with purple and red primroses. Jordan pushed off. The skateboard rolled, its rhythmic and gritty sound filling my ears. He executed three kick turns, then glanced over his shoulder. "Bye, Lois. Love your pants."

I gawked at my inside–out Cal pants. "I wore them this way on purpose!"

Jordan grinned. "Sure you did!"

My eye roll might have distracted him from the mortification flaming across my cheeks. But I doubted it, given the impish glee sparkling in his lake-blue eyes before he twisted away to navigate the blacktop ahead.

Jordan glided down the driveway, his knees slightly bent, his arms loose at his sides. I waited until he had disappeared from sight before I closed the door. Some invisible force pulled me back to the living room. My feet may have touched the floor — I wasn't sure. I couldn't feel my legs. Dazed, I plopped down on the couch.

A few pieces of folded binder paper on the coffee table caught my eye. My heart jackhammered as I picked them up.

Evie. I know you hate math. Thought this might help. (I made copies for myself.) Call or email me if you have any questions. See ya, Lab Partner. -J.

I blinked down at the two pages. Step by step, Jordan had explained independent and dependent variables and diagramming. He'd even drawn a couple of graphs with little dialogue bubbles off to the side explaining various aspects of the x-y coordinate plane.

The spell had worked.

Which meant, I realized as a slow burn gnawed at my stomach, that Parvani's love spell might be equally successful.

CHAPTER FIFTEEN

The next morning, I dreamt Jordan and I were about seventeen, and racing down Main Street in Disneyland. The sun shone, corny music played in the background, and the smell of popcorn filled the air. The scene shifted, and we sat next to each other on a boat ride. On the curve before the big waterfall, Jordan leaned close. This was it. The big kiss. I parted my lips, my body one giant tingle of anticipation, and — the phone woke me.

"No!" I cried into the pillow.

I staggered to my desk, plunged my hand into a pile of papers, and unearthed the cordless phone. Parvani's name showed on the caller ID.

"Hey," I said. "I'm so sorry. I forgot to call you back last night." Actually, I'd been too upset to call, but what's one more lie between best friends?

"You're forgiven." Parvani sounded worried. "Was Zhù in Yearbook yesterday? He made it to History and Honors Geometry, but I didn't see him on the field after school."

My conversation with Señora Allende flashed in my mind, along with a half-dozen worrisome thoughts. "No, I didn't see him." *But I wasn't there the whole time.*

"I hope he's okay. Maybe I'll text him."

"Yeah, you should. Good luck."

"Thanks. Bye."

Zhù. Zhù. Zhù. I tapped the receiver against my lips. *The longer he's absent, the more Parvani will realize how much she cares about him. The more she realizes, the less inclined she'll be to perform a love spell involving Jordan.* I had some serious work to do.

"Evie, you're running late. Get moving!"

I saluted my bedroom door and Mom's voice beyond it. The woman was not a morning person. She must have been a mind reader though, because when I dragged my carcass out to the kitchen, Mickey Mouse-shaped waffles awaited.

This was going to be a good day. On impulse, I went back to my room and changed into a daffodil-colored top. Parvani — who would watch every fashion reality show if given the time — had designed it. It had a cool, asymmetrical neckline and what she called "bracelet sleeves," which meant the sleeves were three-quarters length to show off your jewelry. Too bad I didn't own any.

Before leaving, I crouched on the floor and made sure the dirty clothes still hid the spell book. When I flipped back my mud-splattered jeans, the grimoire hissed foul-smelling brimstone.

"Stop it!" I ordered. "I'll be back as soon as I can. Behave." My heart did a heavy metal drum solo as I closed the door behind me.

Since we were running late, Mom took the shortcut down Lucas. Weak rays of sunlight caused steam to rise from puddles on the street. I shivered and crossed my arms against my torso. Three more houses, then the stop sign, then the car engine would be warm enough so Mom could turn on the heater.

Up ahead, I spotted Salem walking alongside the road, her body bent beneath the weight of her backpack. Her breath formed tiny clouds. A long black sweater billowed beneath her backpack and slate-colored leggings encased her matchstick legs.

"Mom, pull over. It's Sarah."

Mom swerved the Volvo to the curb as if she were a police officer cutting off a suspect. If I had been Salem, I would have screamed or had a heart attack. Instead, she froze and reached for the pentacle keychain on her backpack.

I jumped out. "Hey! Want a ride?"

Her face relaxed and she released the five-pointed star. "Sure. Thanks."

"Sarah, this is my mom," I said as Salem crawled into the backseat.

"Thanks for stopping," Salem said. "My mom's car has a flat tire and we didn't discover it until after Dad was halfway to San Francisco."

"Oh no," Mom said in her most sympathetic voice. "You should have called us."

"Next time." Salem opened up her backpack and pulled out a yellow folder with doodles all over the cover. I recognized it from English. "Do you think we'll have a quiz today?"

I flashed on the less-than-stellar grade Salem had gotten on the last one. "I think we're going to get the first drafts of our compositions back."

Salem sighed. "I wish I was as good at English as you are."

"Trust me, you're way better at math. Everyone is."

Mom did a California slowdown at the stop sign and switched on the heat. Warmth kicked out of the dusty vents with a low roar. Four more turns, and we reached Parvani's wrought iron gate. As it hummed open in a graceful sweep, I said, "Sit by me in English. I'll be your critique partner."

Salem's jaw dropped. Her kohl-rimmed, blue-gray eyes widened a bit. "Awesome. Thanks."

Mom's silent approval wrapped around me like a love cloud.

Parvani appeared preoccupied as she emerged from her house and headed for the car. When she opened the door, the soothing sounds of the Tuscan fountain trickled in. Parvani raised her backpack to throw it, stopping at the last moment when she noticed Salem. "Oh, hey."

"Guess who we found walking to school," I said.

"Flat tire," Salem added.

"Bummer." Parvani dropped her backpack on the floor mat, settled in, and buckled up.

Salem shoved her yellow folder into her backpack. "Nice mansion."

"Thanks." The warmth from the car steamed Parvani's glasses. She pulled them off and blinked.

"Did you reach Zhù?" I asked.

"No. I didn't!" Parvani sounded incredulous and worried. She didn't have much experience with Zhù ignoring her. Just Jordan. *Something she might want to consider.*

Once we reached school and said good-bye to Mom, we crossed the football field. A pack of senior girls shivering in clingy tops, mini-skirts, and flip-flops did a double take when they saw us. A twinge of doubt snaked into my brain. Would hanging out with Salem make me seem like a loser?

I checked to make sure the lump from my film canister necklace wasn't too obvious. *Hmm.* Maybe I was the one endangering Salem's reputation. Parvani, with her perfect ballerina posture and exquisite couture clothes, appeared oblivious. She kept looking around, and for once I didn't think she was searching for Jordan.

Salem and I exchanged glances.

In English, I repaid Salem for the talisman and makeup by helping her improve her essay on Guy Montag in *Fahrenheit 451.* I felt sure she'd get an A on it now. My do-gooder endorphin glow carried over into Gym, even though Jordan and I were assigned opposite teams in Capture the Flag.

"I saw Zhù," Parvani whispered. Behind us, the rest of the yellow team took position. We were caught up front near the border. Prisoner material. Dead meat. "He wouldn't tell me why he missed Yearbook and Spanish."

"Maybe he had to go to the doctor for some embarrassing ailment." *You know, like lovesickness.*

"Do you think so?" Parvani's brows knotted.

Deep within Red Flag territory, Jordan angled his head at me. Parvani didn't notice. I decided to pounce while she was preoccupied with Zhù. "About the love spell..."

Coach's whistle seared my eardrums. Someone grabbed me from behind and I screamed.

"Evan!" Parvani yelled. "We're on the same team. Let her go!"

Tommy Deitch barreled toward us. I struggled to break out of Evan's grasp.

Parvani grabbed Evan's arm and pulled. "You can't imprison your own teammate."

Evan ignored her. He walked me forward, his vile arms still locked around me. Clearly he planned to hand me over to Tommy, who plowed through the red team, his feral gaze locked on me.

I stomped on Evan's foot so hard I heard a sickening snap. *Oh no.* I hoped he'd been standing on a twig.

Evan howled and released me. Parvani let go of his arm so fast she stumbled back, just as Tommy crossed the border. A bewildered look passed over Tommy's face as Evan crumpled to the ground.

I swiped Tommy across the chest. "Tag! You're captured." Then I looked down at Evan. All color had drained from his face. Fear rose like bile, burning my throat.

"Man, Evie!" Evan gasped.

The whistle blew. Coach stormed toward us. "What's going on here?"

Parvani defended me. "Evan accosted Evie."

Coach Willis glanced at me, then Evan, who rocked back and forth clutching his foot, his teeth clenched.

"Evan, I'm…"

Coach cut me off. "Deitch, help him up and take him to the school nurse."

Tommy tried, but Evan seemed unable to stand. I bit my thumbnail. A growing case of guilt and worry gnawed at my conscience.

Jordan joined the circle of kids clustered around us. He helped Coach lift Evan, and then he and Tommy clasped forearms to create a makeshift chair. As they carried Evan to the office, I tugged the brim of Dad's cap low across my forehead. Still, Coach's gaze burned into me.

My mind flashed on the upcoming yearbook assignments. Weren't football play-offs coming up? And I'd just wounded one of Coach's best players. I held my breath, waiting for him to mete out my punishment. Detention? Suspension? Trial by water?

Coach blew the whistle. "Resume sides, people."

****

At lunch, Jordan caught up with Parvani and me outside Mr. Ross's room. "Evan just texted me from the hospital. They're waiting for the doc to read the x-rays, but Evan thinks he'll be sidelined for the rest of the season." Jordan raked his fingers through his hair. "The big play-off game is right before Halloween."

I fought the urge to barf.

"He deserved it," Parvani said.

"Do you think I'll get kicked out of school?"

"No," Parvani said. "I think the freshmen will give you a medal."

"They sell fake ones at the party store. I say we start a write-in campaign. Evie for School Enforcer." It was Zhù, grinning and cracking a joke. Reality as I knew it tilted on its axis.

Parvani broke into a huge smile. Zhù and Jordan flanked her. I waited for the hyperventilation to begin.

"You guys want to work on the HG homework?" Zhù asked.

"Sure," she said.

"Home and Garden?" I asked.

"Honors Geometry," Jordan explained. "Miss Ravenwood piled it on again." He nodded to Parvani and Zhù. "You two go ahead. I'll stay with Evie, like, until the police come for her."

"Stop!" I swatted his shoulder and then leaned back against classroom wall.

"Later, then." Zhù cast a questioning look at Parvani.

She pushed her designer frames up the bridge of her nose then threw Jordan a coy look. "Text me if she needs bail money."

Zhù expelled a long breath.

Jordan nodded. "Right after Evie and I prepare for Biology."

I gaped, which probably wasn't too attractive. Since I was apparently invisible, it hardly mattered.

Jordan watched them leave, then tipped up my cap brim. He gazed so deeply into my eyes, my stomach fluttered. "Did you find my note?"

With his face so close, my concentration wobbled. "Yes. Thank you." The memory warmed me all over. I struggled to focus on something other than Jordan's lips. "I'm so sorry about Evan, and about hurting your chances in the play-offs."

Jordan raked his fingers through his hair again. "We'll manage somehow. But if I get creamed out there..."

"I will so never forgive myself." I wondered if *Teen Wytche* had a protection spell for JV running backs. "Do we have biology homework?"

"Nah." He joined me against the wall, standing so close our shoulders touched. All my nerve endings jumped to attention. "I just wanted to have lunch with the most notorious girl in school."

"So now I have a reputation," I teased. "You shouldn't be consorting with the enemy. Evan is kinda your friend."

Jordan pivoted with athletic grace and faced me again. His eyebrows twitched. He leaned closer, his breath warm upon my cheek. "Consorting, eh?"

I pushed him, his shoulders strong and solid beneath his fleece sweatshirt. A blush heated my throat. "You know what I mean."

Jordan's expression grew serious. "Evan's not so awful when you get him away from Tommy. Even so, he's more of a teammate than a friend, especially after today. Man, Evie. Once everyone started moving on the field, I couldn't see you at all. If I had, I would have taken him down."

My stomach flutter morphed into a delicious full body tingle. "Seriously?"

His brow crinkled. "Of course. But in a way where he could still play football." He flashed one of his dazzling, I'm-playing-with-you smiles.

Wow. If I don't get expelled, arrested, or burn for eternity because I broke Evan's foot, this will go down as one of my best days ever.

CHAPTER SIXTEEN

No one in remedial math — okay, Algebra B — liked Evan MacDonald.

I felt wretched. After all, I had caused serious harm. And even though Evan had started it, I still worried about the karmic repercussion. Or worse, what if my name was announced over the school P.A. system? Then I'd have to do the perp walk to the office.

I pulled Dad's hat low over my eyes.

No sign of Zhù in Yearbook. I had just seen him an hour before. My heart hip-hopped. If he didn't show up pronto, I'd have to do the club shots. I kept glancing at the door, half listening while Miss Roberts gave everyone their assignments.

"Evie." Miss Robert's voice cut through my spiraling panic. "I'd like to speak with you outside for a sec."

I reached for the orange topaz in my pocket. *Here it comes. I'm expelled. I bet the Volvo is already in the parking lot.*

"The first set of pages are due in seven days," Miss Roberts said when we reached the bottom of the ramp. "As photo editor..."

"I know. I'm on top of it." *Maybe word from the hospital hasn't reached the principal yet.* "Hallie has been taking candids of the teachers, and Zhù should be here any minute to shoot the drama club. They're rehearsing this period. I'm going to work on cropping the photos from Diversity Overnight…"

"I need you to switch assignments with Zhù for the rest of the semester. You'll take the photos and download them. Zhù will work from home on cropping. In January you can switch back."

"But…"

Miss Roberts put her hand on my shoulder. "You're an A student, Evie."

"Except for math." *And probably Biology.*

"Still. You don't want to fail Yearbook." She held up a camera. I began to sweat. Panic overloaded my brain.

"You are an experienced, award-winning photographer. You're the only freshman to ever be offered an editorship. I took a chance on you."

Hot tears threatened to breach my eyes. Dad would have been so proud I'd made photo editor. He would be so disappointed if I let down Miss Roberts. *I should let Zhù flunk Spanish.*

"Tell you what," Miss Roberts said. "Take Mia with you to the performing arts center. You can start training her to become a photographer."

"Mia?" *The girl who wears three skirts at a time and looks like she just stepped off a gypsy caravan?* "But she's in charge of copy."

"And she won't have any captions to write if no one takes pictures." Miss Roberts pressed the camera into my hand. "Wait here. I'll go get her."

My thoughts flew like leaves tossed in the wind. *Where's Zhù, and why will he be working from home? And why give the camera to me if Mia is going to be taking the pictures?*

Mia must have been waiting on the other side of the classroom door, because she skipped down the ramp as soon as Miss Roberts disappeared.

"Cool top." Mia folded a stick of bright green gum into her mouth and stuffed the wrapper in her skirt pocket. "My boyfriend is in the play. The first performance is tonight, you know."

"I didn't know. I mean, I forgot. Dress rehearsal, of course." No wonder I had assigned the photos to be shot today. The actors would be in costume and makeup.

"This will be our one chance to take the pictures," Mia said. "I'd sure hate to blow it."

"Yeah, me too." The top of my scalp began to feel weird.

Mia walked with a quick, bouncy gait, her skirts rustling. I almost broke into a trot trying to keep up. Which was pretty difficult, considering my head had opened up like a can of diced tomatoes and I was about to float out of my body.

Mia chattered on and on about her boyfriend, Nazario, who played the role of Lenny in the school production, *Of Mice and Men.* Her words buzzed around my overwrought brain, anchoring me, blocking the panic gathering like a storm. Her insider gossip about the cast and crew — no one respected the director — carried us to the double doors of the performing arts center.

Mia spit her gum into the foil wrapper and then tossed it into the trashcan. "How's my breath?" she asked, making a *hah* sound.

"Fine." *Please! We're here to work, not hook up.*

She reached for the silver door handle and her colorful plastic bangles rocketed toward her wrist with a series of tiny clacks. Before I could stop her, we were inside.

Near darkness cloaked the auditorium, save for the warm glare of yellow-filtered spotlights illuminating the stage. The set designers had transformed it into a barn, complete with rustic-looking wooden walls. A couple of bridles hung on hooks, and someone had leaned a shovel against the side wall. The dusty smell of hay filled the room.

Mia pulled a spiral notepad out of her pocket and took off for the steps leading to the stage.

"Mia, wait!" I held up the digital. "You forgot the camera."

She never stopped. If anything, the wretched little gypsy sped up. When she reached the black curtain leading to the wings, the light from one of the spots glinted off her gold hoop earring, and then she disappeared.

I contemplated murder. I had already broken bones today. It wasn't such a long slide to wring Mia's neck. I pulled the talisman from under my sweater. The milky crystal within the film canister rattled reassuringly. I forced myself to breathe in and out.

A hulking boy dressed in work clothes — Mia's boyfriend, I presumed — walked onstage carrying a small stuffed dog. A cloud of dust rose as he plopped onto the hay and settled into a kneeling position with the toy dog in front of him.

Where was Mia? This was the pivotal scene. Do or die time.

Keeping an eye on Nazario, I gravitated toward the center of the front row. *I can't breathe.* Nazario petted the little dog. *I'm not going to take a picture. I'm just walking with a camera.*

Nazario's soft, deep voice washed over me in the darkness. I averted my gaze when he pretended to kill the stuffed dog.

A senior girl, Pilar Somebody, crept onstage, an open script in her hand. Her straight raven hair grazed the pale puff sleeves of her costume, a simple housedress. The light caught her red Marilyn Monroe lipstick.

I felt the blood drain from my face.

I placed the camera on the nearest chair and rotated Dad's hat so the brim faced backwards. Grabbing the camera with one hand and the back of the chair with the other, I climbed up. Dizzy, feet numb, I eyed the stage. Nazario stood and kicked some hay over the "dead" pup. Pilar and Nazario both started talking, each lost in their character's story. Nazario, as Lenny, said something about liking soft things.

A sense of foreboding shivered down my arms.

Pilar angled toward Nazario and told him to touch her hair. The play of light shadowed Pilar's thick eyelashes against her flawless, dusky skin. She dropped her script. The pages ruffled. My nerves prickled. The film canister talisman weighed against my too-fast heart.

I gave the wings a furtive glance. Still no Mia.

The topaz pressed against the thin cotton of my pocket. I raised the camera to my eye and pressed the shutter release. Nazario's hands closed around Pilar's neck and her Bambi eyes widened with pretend fear.

I held my breath.

Pilar plummeted to the hay in a convincing death drop. Nazario dropped to his knees and I captured his shocked expression. The boy could act. No wonder Mia had raved. I kept shooting.

The scene ended and back in the tech booth, someone killed the lights.

"Excellent," the director boomed from one of the back rows.

Startled, I almost teetered off the chair.

"Now do it again without your script, please." The lights came on. "We should be way past open scripts, people."

A little dizzy, I climbed down.

"They cast a girl as the ranch boss," Mia whispered, appearing at my side like a gypsy ghost. "Do you want me to take her picture?"

I hesitated. "Sure." I handed Mia the camera and wiped my sweaty palms on the front of my jeans.

"I push this button, right?"

"Yes," I said through clenched teeth. "Try to get a group scene with as many actors as possible on stage."

Mia blinked yes and was off.

I sank into the chair, exhausted. My arm trembled as I clasped the talisman. I'd done it. I had taken the shot, lots of shots. Dad would have been proud.

I owed Salem. Big time.

CHAPTER SEVENTEEN

The jeans on the blonde ahead of me in the girls' bathroom were so long they trailed on the ground, and had become frayed and torn. Exactly how my nerves felt. Stepped on. Ragged. My momentary elation and relief at taking the photos morphed into a serious desire to curl up and nap. I didn't want Mr. Esenberg to pick on me in Science. And I didn't want anyone to think I could take pictures now, just because I had managed to do it once.

I also didn't want Jordan to think his lab partner had freaked out again, so I dashed on some Nearly Nude lipstick and dragged myself to class.

"Hey, Evie." Jordan sounded casual, but I had a sparkly feeling he'd been watching for me.

"Hey." I collapsed into the empty seat in front of him.

"Everything okay?"

I flashed him my best post-braces smile. "Sure."

He scrunched up his face as if unconvinced. Luckily, Mr. Esenberg arrived, halting further communication.

About ten minutes into class, while Mr. Esenberg wrote on the board, I heard Jordan slide his feet under my desk. My breath wedged in my throat as the tips of his size nine high-performance sneakers nudged the heels of my shoes. Could the girl in front of me hear my heart thudding? Should I move my feet forward?

My feet tingled and refused to move. A blush blazed across my cheeks. I struggled to pay attention to Mr. Esenberg without making eye contact. Forty minutes passed, the bell blared, and I had no idea what had transpired. *Hopefully, my notes will make sense. I think I took notes.*

Jordan slid his feet back and thudded his book closed. We both bent down and reached for our backpacks. His leaned against mine. Our hands brushed and our heads were so close I could smell his herbal shampoo.

Students walked past us. I'm sure some of them were talking to each other or pulling out their cell phones. But it all faded away along with the smell of chalk, highlighters, and sweat. Everything receded except the warmth of Jordan's skin, his cinnamon gum-scented breath, and the heart-stopping rush sprinting up my arm.

"Evie?"

We jerked apart. Seeing Parvani in the doorway looking hurt and shocked snapped my senses into hyper focus. Conversations sounded extra loud. Colors seemed too bright. It felt like a movie had started, full blast, in a hushed theater.

I grabbed my backpack, stood up, and tried to look innocent. "Hey," I said, a little too loudly.

Parvani adjusted her designer frames further up her nose. "My mom just called. She's going to pick me up and drive me to the hospital. We have to drop off the pillows I made."

Parvani glanced at Jordan as he rose from his chair and stood beside me. I wondered if he knew she made heart-shaped pillows for women who'd had mastectomies. The pillows kept seatbelts from rubbing against the stitches, or something. *I should think about building my résumé for college. Besides, I've heard helping others alleviates depression.*

"Could you tell your mom I don't need a ride?" I heard a definite edge to her voice.

"Sure."

Jordan slung his backpack over his shoulder. "How's it going?"

Parvani acted startled, like she had just noticed him. But her voice softened. "Oh. Hello, Jordan." To me, she said, "Thank you. Goodbye."

Unease spider-walked down my spine. I stepped toward her, trying to close the chasm that had sprung up between us. "Talk to you later."

Parvani didn't reply. She just left, her long black hair swinging across her shoulders.

Jordan fell into step behind me. "Did I miss something? Is she all right?"

He sounded like the old Jordan — the sensitive, pre-Smash Heads Jordan I had grown up with. Since I couldn't give him the obvious and correct answer, I spun through possible alternatives.

Loud static from the school's public address system blasted my eardrums, followed by the school secretary's voice. "Evie O'Reilly. Please come to the office. Evie O'Reilly. Please come to the office."

I froze. My flushed cheeks grew hotter. Every kid crossing the field had heard my name. Cold fear formed bricks in my stomach. What if something had happened to Mom?

"Maybe Evan's parents called the principal," Jordan said.

The blood sluiced from head and pooled in my feet.

"Come on," Jordan said. "I'll walk with you."

As we headed toward the office, Jordan's cell phone vibrated. He checked the phone number displayed then tapped the screen.

"Hey, Mom." After listening a sec, he said, "I don't know. We're walking to the office right now."

I chewed my thumbnail. I had already lost one parent. I couldn't face losing another one. What if Mom had gotten into a car accident or something?

"Okay. I'll tell Evie. See you in about five minutes." He tapped the phone. "Mom heard the announcement while she was waiting in the car. She says she hopes everything is okay."

"That was nice of her." *Great. Even the parents know something is wrong.*

We rounded the corner. A few juniors milled about in front of the lockers across from the office. "Perfect. I have an audience."

Jordan took my hand, sending a jolt of warmth and fresh shivers up my arm. "Come on."

My heart swelled. I knew Jordan had to be somewhere before practice. His mom was waiting. And I was pretty sure rumors we were a couple would scream through the eleventh grade by tomorrow morning. I just hoped it didn't reach the ninth grade and Parvani.

Jordan released my hand and opened the door for me. Relief flooded every pore when I saw Mom. She stood in front of a boy who was taping an orange poster to the wall. It screamed *Halloween Dance* in black letters, dripping with what was supposed to be blood.

The vein at Mom's temple throbbed and her arms were crossed. I didn't care. She was okay. Nothing had happened to her. Which meant something was about to happen to *me*.

"Good luck," Jordan said.

I nodded and watched him leave before going to Mom and giving her a quick hug.

"Mrs. O'Reilly? Evie?" Mrs. Scroggins sounded curt, like big trouble lay ahead. "This way please." She led us back to a windowless office.

Principal Sanders rose from his chair behind his battered desk, cutting off his conversation with Miss Gaya, who sat on a blue plastic chair next to Coach Willis.

I reached for the topaz in my pocket.

Principal Sanders extended his hand. "Mrs. O'Reilly, thank you for coming." Mom shook his hand. He nodded to me. "Evie."

"Hey, Principal Sanders." I tried to not stare at his toupee.

He gestured toward Miss Gaya. "Mrs. O'Reilly, this is Grace Gaya, our school counselor."

Mom nodded. "We spoke on the phone."

"Yes," Miss Gaya said.

"And Coach Willis."

Mom and the coach shook hands.

"Evie, Mrs. O'Reilly, please sit down."

We did as Principal Sanders commanded. He sat as well, flattening his maroon tie against his abs as he sat. "I understand there was an incident in P.E. today," he said in a grave tone. "Coach Willis has already filled me in, but Evie, I'd like you to tell us about it."

I'd rather go home, crawl into bed, and pull the covers over my head. But everyone was watching me, so I said, "I didn't mean to hurt Evan, but…" I told them about him grabbing me and refusing to let go. "So I stomped on his foot to get him to release me."

The room fell silent. The only sound I heard over my heart tripping was Coach's deep sigh. I sensed the tide rising against me. Desperate, I added, "It's something my dad taught me to do in case I was ever attacked from behind."

Mom squeezed my hand. Principal Sanders glanced at Miss Gaya. The counselor shifted in her seat and angled her body toward me.

Principal Sanders folded his hands on the desktop. "Evan MacDonald's father called me from the hospital. Evan has two broken bones in his foot." Principal Sanders's toothbrush-like eyebrows shot up.

"I'm so sorry." *Please don't expel me.*

The wall clock ticked. I hadn't noticed it before. The room warmed and grew stuffy. Principal Sanders angled his head. "Some might argue Evan is the injured party."

I tightened my hold on Mom's hand.

"Surely you don't condone Evan's actions," Mom said. "My daughter acted in self-defense."

"We can't be sure Evan intended any real harm."

"Of course he intended harm!" Heat exploded throughout my body. "I have witnesses."

Mom leaned forward and cast her patented death stare at Principal Sanders. Her voice grew glacial. "Compare Evie's school record to Evan's and I'm sure it will become clear which child has the history of violence and bullying."

"We do not endorse bullying or violence of any kind at Jefferson High," Principal Sanders said. "Our bylaws require us to suspend any student who harms another..."

"He wouldn't let go!" I shrieked.

"She was assaulted," Mom protested, annunciating every syllable.

Miss Gaya uncrossed her legs and made a placating motion with her hand. "Mrs. O'Reilly..."

Principal Sanders cut her off. "I realize there were mitigating circumstances. Evan will be suspended for one week.

Unfortunately, we must also suspend Evie. But" — he held up his hand like a stop sign again — "just for the rest of the week, two days. Consider it a cooling off period."

"Which will appease the school board and the MacDonalds," Coach added under his breath. "Though I'm still short a defensive lineman."

A dangerous edge crept into Mom's voice. "I don't care about appeasing the MacDonalds. Their son is a bully. It's outrageous to suspend Evie for defending herself."

I stood up. "Everyone saves face this way, Mom. I'm fine with it."

"It will go on your permanent record," Mom argued. "It could harm your chances of getting into college."

"I'll submit a letter in your favor, Evie." Miss Gaya glanced at Principal Sanders, daring him to stop her. "I'll explain the circumstances."

"Thank you, Miss Gaya." Mom rose. "If Evan or Tommy Deitch cross the line again, I'll sue the school for placing my daughter in harm's way. I don't care if the boys are two of your star athletes. You're supposed to provide a safe environment."

Principal Sanders stood up. "I understand."

"Thank you," I said to the room in general. My gaze met Miss Gaya's. She nodded.

Mom and I fled out the door. We were halfway across the field when Mom stopped. "Where's Parvani?"

"Her mother picked her up. They had to drop off some pillows."

"Oh, thank goodness."

I slipped my hand in Mom's. Dad's emerald sparkled. "Thanks, Mom. You're the best."

"You, too. And when I calm down about Evan, you can tell me about the lipstick you're wearing."

CHAPTER EIGHTEEN

When we got home, I wiped off my lipstick and hid all the tubes, except Nearly Nude. I figured better to offer a token sacrifice than to lose my entire stash. Then I waited for Mom to call me on it.

Baby kept running to the front door, then coming back to my room and nudging me. Wallowing in worry and depression didn't fly in Dog World. I gave up and grabbed her leash, and we took off. We got two blocks from home when the sky darkened into an ominous gray and it started to sprinkle. I dragged Baby home.

I had just crawled onto my bed when the phone rang. I debated letting it go unanswered. But, just in case it was Jordan, I followed the noise to my desk. Miraculously, the device rested in its charger for a change.

"Hello?"

"I told you to throw a glamour, not get busted."

"Hey, Sal — Sarah."

"Hey. What happened?"

"I broke Evan MacDonald's foot in Gym."

"Are you *serious?*"

"Afraid so. I feel awful about it. Plus, I got a two-day suspension."

"O'Reilly, you rock! Can you take out Tommy as well?"

I laughed. "I'll think about it." The beanbag chair squished as it engulfed me. "I took some photos in Yearbook today."

"No way!"

"Your talisman helped. So thanks. I owe you."

"Cool."

The line went quiet. I thought maybe she was calling from a cell phone and I had lost her. Then her voice came back, sort of hesitant and nervous. "I could use a favor."

I sat up straighter, every cell wary. "What?"

"You know the test we're supposed to have in English tomorrow?"

My shoulders relaxed as I remembered her quiz score. It reminded me way too much of my math woes. "Want to study together?"

"For real?" She sounded relieved. "That would be great."

"Come over. Maybe if you're here, Mom will forget to confiscate the lipstick she caught me wearing."

"Dude! When you get busted, everything hits the fan."

"Pretty much."

"I'll call my mom at work, then walk over."

"Okay. See ya." I hung up and surveyed the remnants of my spell casting. The magic circle resembled a kiddie party thanks to the troll and tiara. I stuffed them on a shelf in my wicker hutch, then carried the poppy plate to the kitchen.

Salem arrived about fifteen minutes later, appearing windblown and hunched under the weight of her backpack. "I suck at English."

"I suck worse at math." It seemed to put her at ease. "We can work in my room if you don't mind the mess."

"Lead on, soldier." Salem saluted, then, when I gave her a puzzled look, she pointed to Dad's camouflage hat.

"Oh, right." I saluted back, but when we got to my room, I did something I never do. I took off the hat.

Salem squinted at my strawberry "outgrowth," as Mom calls it. "Major roots."

"I know. I need to see a colorist."

"My cousin is in cosmetology school. She needs the practice. I could ask her, if you'd like."

"Awesome. That would be great."

We settled onto the cleaner of my twin beds so Baby wouldn't bother us, and pulled out our English notebooks. "We're going to have to identify the Greek and Latin roots of the vocabulary words, so we need to know their origins as well as their meaning."

Salem groaned.

"It gets worse. I think we are going to have to write a persuasive essay about one of the books from the summer reading list. Which ones did you read?"

"Gregory Macquire's *Wicked*, and *The Bell Jar*. You?"

"Jane Austen, *The Count of Monte Cristo,* and *All Quiet on the Western Front.*" And four more, but I figured, why freak her out?

An hour flew by as we worked together. We both jumped when Mom stuck her head in the door. "Evie…?" She saw Salem and stopped.

"Mom, you remember Sarah."

Mom had a dazed, it's-three-days-until-deadline look. "Hi, Sarah. I was just about to ask Evie if she'd like pizza delivered. You're welcome to join us."

"Thanks." Salem gave me a questioning look to see if I was okay with the invitation.

"Great," I said.

Mom glanced down at the notebooks in our laps. If she was surprised to see me studying, she hid it well. "Double cheese with a thick crust?"

"Sounds great," Salem said. "I'll call my folks and let them know."

"Tell them I'll give you a ride home."

"Thanks, Mrs. O'Reilly." Salem pulled out her cell phone and punched the speed dial.

"You're welcome." Mom flexed her hands several times as she left.

My house phone rang. *Parvani.* I picked it up and answered it just as Salem started talking to her dad.

"Evie?"

"Hey, Parvani." I strained to hear her over Salem.

"Who's in the background?"

"Sarah Miller came over."

There was a slight pause, where I swore I could hear the synapses sparking in Parvani's busy brain. "Well, I was just calling to see what happened with Evan."

"I got suspended." I explained the whole thing.

Parvani sounded frosty. "If you can't go to school, then why are you studying with Salem?"

I figured Salem wouldn't want anyone to know about her struggles in English. But I also flashed on Parvani's hurt expression when she had seen me with Jordan. Great. Another lose-lose situation.

"I still have to do the homework and I'll have to make up the tests." I glanced at Salem. She had hung up her cell, and watched me with a worried look on her face.

"So, how did things go with the pillows?" I asked Parvani.

"Fine. Look, I have to go. I'll talk to you later."

"Why don't you join us…?" I started to say, but the phone went dead.

"Everything okay?" Salem asked.

"More or less." *Mostly less.* I hated being stuck in the middle between Parvani and Jordan. *And now what? Parvani's mad because Salem came over?*

Worry knotted my stomach. Thanks to Evan, I'd be stuck at home for the next two days and unable to counter the gossip mill. Of course I had no good explanation for why Jordan had taken my hand. Actually, I had an excellent explanation, but Parvani wouldn't like it.

Salem threw a bounty hunter squint again, then slid off the bed and stretched. Something in the hutch must have caught her eye, because she walked over to look at it. Her toe flipped the hidden spell book out from beneath the dirty clothes.

Salem kneeled on the floor and pulled out the grimoire. "Dude!" She brushed her hand across the plum-colored leather. "Where did you get this?"

"Well-Read Books." I dropped to my knees beside her. *Unbelievable.* A raised, leafy, silver vine had sprouted at the bottom corner near the spine, and fanned out across the front cover.

"I didn't know they had a rare books section." She skimmed through it, stopping when she encountered yellow streaks. "You *highlighted* it?" She sounded horrified.

"I didn't. Parvani did. But it was an ordinary book when she highlighted it."

Oops.

Salem narrowed her eyes again. "What do you mean?"

I hesitated, searching for a cover story or way to deflect her attention. But Salem's pale, kohl-rimmed eyes bored into me like police spotlights. I broke. "It was a regular paperback book when I bought it, but it keeps changing."

"Are you serious?"

"Deadly serious." I winced as the words left my mouth, and I glanced at Dad's cap. "For instance, the silver part wasn't here yesterday."

"Holy Goddess. Any idea what's making it change?"

Bad mojo? "I don't know, but it creeps me out."

Salem sat cross-legged and flipped through a few more pages, tracing her finger along several of the highlighted sentences. After a few minutes, she glanced up. "What are you and Parvani up to?"

I chewed my thumbnail, something I hadn't done since I was ten.

"Look," Salem said. "This is serious magick. You shouldn't do anything until you've read the whole book. And *then* you shouldn't do anything without consulting an experienced practitioner."

"You mean someone like Miss Ravenwood?"

"You better stay clear of her. Did you ever find your parents' yearbooks?"

"I haven't had a chance to look." Miss Ravenwood and her broomstick had flown off my radar with all the other things going on. I glanced at the troll and tiara. "I read some of the first part. It seems pretty harmless."

"It can be harmless, if you do it right and take certain precautions. If you ignore the warnings or forget a step, there could be serious consequences. *Karmic* consequences."

The worry knot in my stomach grew like a population of rats without inhibitors.

"For instance," Salem said. "Look at this."

The book fell open to a section on love spells. My heart stopped. No yellow highlights. Clearly, Parvani hadn't read this far yet. "Love Spells. Perform during the new moon to full moon, or on the full moon." I made a mental note to check the calendar.

Salem skimmed her finger down the spidery list of correspondences. "Colors: red and white." *Gee, what a surprise.* "Herbs and plants: apple, barley, Brazil nuts, ginger. Planets: Venus. Day of the week: Friday." *Figures.* "Flowers: Coltsfoot? Daffodil, daisy, lavender, rose, etc."

Salem's finger, with its chipped black nail polish, halted. She read aloud, "'Warning. Never try to bind someone to you through magick. Such misuse of the Craft will have dire consequences in this life and beyond. A love attained through magick is no love.'"

"Why tell someone how to perform a love spell if it is going to curse them for all eternity? And what about people like Parvani? She believes in reincarnation."

Baby, who was quite fond of Parvani, whimpered from the doorway.

"The book is trying to warn you how you should and shouldn't perform a love spell." She pointed to another line and read it aloud. "'Do not direct your spell at a specific person. Instead, write down the qualities you seek in a true love.'"

My heart somersaulted. I read further. "'Do nay harm'." I was not getting a warm, fuzzy feeling about this.

"The Wicca creed includes 'Be silent', but I'll break it just this once," Salem said. "I've been studying the Craft for a year now. So if you need any help…"

"Thanks. But I'm going to try and talk Parvani out of it. This time I'll make her listen."

"Then this isn't about trying to contact your dad?"

I reeled back on my heels, shocked. "No, of course not. I hadn't even thought of such a thing."

"Good, because you need to take heed before you try to contact the Other Side. Especially this time of year." I must have appeared as confused as I felt. Salem explained, "Samhain. You know, Halloween. The veil between this world and the spirit world becomes thin."

"Oh." I reached for Dad's cap and anchored it on my head. It reeked of sweat and shampoo, but I imagined it also smelled of all the dangerous countries Dad had photographed.

The doorbell rang, startling me out of my reverie. "Must be the pizza," I said over Baby's barking.

"Maybe it's Parvani." Salem stashed the spell book beneath the discarded clothes.

Rattled, I led the way toward the entry.

Chapter Nineteen

It wasn't Parvani at the door. It was Jordan. My stomach did a rollercoaster climb toward my ribcage, then freefell.

Jordan did a double take when he saw Salem. "Hey," he said to both of us.

"Hey," Salem and I said at the same time. She arched her over-plucked brows and slid me a what's-up-with-the-jock glance.

I felt my face turn dodge ball red. "Jordan sits behind me in Bio," I explained. "We've known each other since preschool."

"He sits in front of me in History." Salem assumed a reproachful tone. "And totally blocks my view of the board."

"Sorry about that." Jordan tousled her hair like she was a five-year old. Salem knocked his hand away. I held my breath, waiting for her to smite him or something. Jordan just grinned and puffed out his chest. "Evie let me do the perp walk to the office with her. She needed a bodyguard, like, in case Evan was waiting to whack her with his crutches."

I swatted his shoulder. My pulse skittered when my hand made contact with his solid bicep.

The pizza guy drove up in a little white truck. "Come in," I told Jordan. Then, to the delivery guy, "Be right back."

Mom emerged from the kitchen with her bulging red wallet in hand. I winced when I noticed all the discount coupons sticking out. "Hi Jordan," she said as she handed the pizza man some cash. "Want to stay for dinner?"

Jordan breathed in the garlicky pizza smell and breathed out the word, "Yes."

Hoping Parvani wouldn't discover us, I rushed everyone to the kitchen. Mom said, "Can you get…?"

"Got it." I pulled another placemat from the drawer. The dark green mats cover a lot of scratches on the table. *Mom should stick to the studio, or be more careful when she works on her greeting cards in the kitchen.*

"So what happened?" Jordan asked as I handed him four sage-colored plates. For the third time, I told about my suspension. "And Evan got a week? Harsh."

Salem came to my defense. "He's a jerk. Besides, he should pay for all the things they didn't catch him at."

"Amen." Mom placed a big glass salad bowl on the table and began tossing mixed greens and feta.

We ate in silence. Baby watched us with bright eyes, no doubt willing us to drop something. After a while, Salem cleared her throat. "Mrs. O'Reilly, I heard you grew up around here."

Mom nodded. "In this house."

"I think my parents were a year ahead of you in school. Maybe you remember them. Mitch Miller and Kimberly Cain?"

Mom lowered her wedge of pizza. "Is your mom a pretty blonde? Petite?"

"Yeah."

Mom broke into a smile. "Now I see the resemblance." Salem blushed.

"Cool." Jordan reached for his third slice of pizza.

Salem stabbed a piece of butter lettuce. "I saw your picture in their yearbook, and Miss Ravenwood's."

Mom's smile vanished.

"No way!" Jordan said. "My math teacher went to Jefferson?"

"Oh, yes." Mom's voice dripped venom. "She had quite a crush on Evie's father."

I almost choked. Mom must have inhaled too much glue while she worked on the cards. Salem and I exchanged sideways glances.

"Wretched," Jordan said. "Did they date or anything?"

Mom's face scrunched like she had an unpleasant taste in her mouth. "I think they went to a Halloween dance during our junior year."

This time I did choke. No one had to do the Heimlich on me, but Salem thumped my back between my shoulder blades, which hurt. When I could breathe again, she nudged me with her foot.

"I heard she's Wiccan or something," Salem said when I stopped coughing. "I wonder if she was practicing back then?"

"Wicca is white magick." Mom's tone suggested Miss Ravenwood dabbled in something quite the opposite.

Every poisoned apple, boiling cauldron, and turn-the-world-into-perpetual-winter scene I'd ever read, or watched at the multiplex flashed before my eyes. Salem nudged me harder. Jordan just blinked several times.

Mom wiped her hands on a paper napkin. "Enough ancient history. I better get back to work." Her chair scraped against the wood floor as she stood. "Sarah, let me know when you're ready for a ride home. I can give you one too, Jordan."

Salem nodded, her mouth full of salad.

Jordan said, "Thanks, Mrs. O."

After Mom headed up to her studio, Salem leaned toward me. "Can you believe it? Miss Ravenwood had a crush on your dad."

"Gross," Jordan said. "What if you were Miss Ravenwood's daughter?"

"Eww." Salem shuddered.

I could think of one advantage—I might have been good at math. *So not worth it.*

Jordan used his fork to chase a piece of arugula around his plate. "Speaking of Halloween dances, either of you planning on going?"

"Not my thing," Salem proclaimed. Given her earlier revelation, I wondered what she did on Halloween. Wasn't it a witch's major holiday?

"Evie?" Jordan drew out my name in a funny way. Before I could answer, he captured a lock of my hair and twirled it around his finger. "Think you can avoid further suspensions so you can go to the dance?"

It almost sounded like Jordan was asking me to the dance. I couldn't tell for sure, so I played it cool. "Well, I don't know, Kent. It depends on whether or not Tommy Deitch stays clear of me."

Salem snorted. Jordan blinked at her, as if he'd forgotten she was there. He released my hair and leaned back in his chair. His hand dropped to the table, about an inch from mine. If either of us moved our pinkies, we'd touch.

"I hate to eat and run," Salem said while carrying her plate to the sink, "but I better go home and feed Einstein."

"Einstein?" Jordan asked. I swear his hand slid a heartbeat closer to mine. "I thought he was, like, way dead."

"Einstein is her dog."

"My sister's dog," Salem clarified. "Amy is away at college. M.I.T. So I'm stuck with dog duty."

"Wretched," Jordan said.

I tried to focus on their banter, but it was difficult with my hand tingling.

"I hate to interrupt your mom when she's working."

I dragged my attention up to Salem. Little worry lines creased her forehead. "Better to interrupt her now than later when she's immersed. I'll help you gather up your stuff." I rose and reached for my water glass, accidentally on purpose brushing Jordan's hand. He was eyeing the last piece of pizza, but his fingers twitched as if he were trying to catch me.

"Why don't you polish off the pizza so I won't have to wrap it?"

"If you insist, Lois." He reached for the slice. I didn't know how he stayed in such great shape. Skateboarding and football must burn lots of calories.

"We'll be right back." Salem linked her arm through mine and dragged me from the kitchen. When we were halfway down the hall, she whispered in my ear. "Lois?"

"It's a Superman joke."

Salem's brow furrowed. "Oh, I get it, Lois Lane and Clark Kent. Jordan Kent. He *so* digs you."

A warm flush crept its way up my throat. "He does not."

"Couldn't you see he wants to take you to the dance?"

I could. One slight problem—my best friend so *digs him.*

We reached my room. Salem giggled. "Just think, *Lois*. Unlike Miss Ravenwood, you don't need to perform a spell to get a date."

"Don't ever say that in front of Parvani."

"Why?" Salem's gaze swung to the pile of clothes concealing the spell book. "Don't tell me. Parvani..."

I clasped her arm. "Please don't tell anyone."

"Of course I won't. Parvani wasn't planning on directing the spell at a particular person, was she?"

I bit my thumbnail. My eyes kind of rolled in their sockets toward the kitchen.

Salem gasped. "Jordan?"

I nodded.

"Holy Goddess. We have to stop her."

CHAPTER TWENTY

I knew Parvani. I couldn't just tell her, "Don't do the spell." I'd have to provide evidence — preferably written, *highlighted* evidence. She already grasped the whole karma thing. I'd just have to prove it applied in this case. And if I failed, maybe the timing of the moon would be on my side. *Otherwise, Parvani might think I'm jealous and want Jordan to myself. Which is true, but beside the point.*

I decided to start with the phases of the moon aspect. After Mom and I dropped off Jordan and Salem, I snuck back to my room, grabbed the calendar off my desk, and pulled out *Teen Wytche*. It was past time for a spell check.

I reread the part about the new moon to the full moon phase being most optimal for casting a love spell. "The full moon is this Saturday," I told Baby. "Parvani will never be ready by then."

I searched the October calendar page for the dark circle representing the next new moon. October 25th. The date seemed too close to Halloween if Parvani was hoping Jordan would ask her to the dance. Maybe I'd get lucky and she'd drop the whole thing.

Maybe Salem and I wouldn't have to pull an intervention.

****

"Evie?"

I willed my face to levitate from my pillow. It wouldn't.

"It's after ten," Mom said from the vicinity of the doorway. "Time to get up."

I peeled one eye open. Light streamed through the white metal mini-blinds. *She must mean ten in the morning.* "Go away."

"Five more minutes, Miss. Walk the dog after breakfast, then come up to my studio. We're on deadline. Since you're suspended, you can help stuff envelopes."

I pictured the stiff plastic display envelopes Mom used to protect her hand-painted greeting cards. "There are child labor laws in this country," I mumbled into the pillow.

"They don't apply to family-run businesses," Mom said in a trilling voice.

Uh oh. Deadline madness has set in.

She came back in five minutes, but it felt like five seconds. "Evie Elizabeth O'Reilly. Get a move on. We have a mortgage to pay."

With a groan, I rolled out of bed and grabbed my sweats from a pile on the floor. *Remind me to kill Evan.* I'd much rather have faced school, Parvani, and the rumor mill than my parents' studio. I'd avoided it since Dad's death. As I climbed the wooden stairs, it felt like I had the Quarter Guardian stones strapped to my legs.

"There you are." Mom swiveled her chair toward me when I opened the door. She'd tied back auburn hair with a black scrunchie. Light sliced through the oversized windows, illuminating a sprinkling of gray strands that hadn't been there before Dad died. "Ready to stuff envelopes?"

"Sure." I took a seat beside her at the worktable. Dad's desk with its seventeen-inch monitor and his darkroom with all its memories were behind me. Even so, my heart clutched. I remembered the darkroom's chemical smells, the tight space, all the hours Dad and I had spent there when I'd been little, before we'd gone digital.

"Want some music?" Mom asked.

"Sure."

Mom punched the play button on the CD player Dad had given her five Christmases ago. After a second, a Beatles song came on. "Don't forget these." Mom handed me a pair of white cotton gloves, so I wouldn't smudge the cards or leave fingerprints on the plastic envelopes.

I reached for a stack of cards, expecting Mom's usual, hand-painted dragonflies in rich emeralds and glittering teal damselflies. They worked amazingly well on everything from birthday cards to sympathy notes. I stared down at the card in my hand. "Mom?"

"I know. They're not what you expected. Do you hate them?"

"No, of course not." I studied the night scene. A pale-skinned woman, dressed in a long black dress, stood before a low-hanging full moon. "It's beautiful. Somber, but beautiful." I checked the back. "Is it mass produced?"

"Yes. From a painting I did — rather, three paintings. I'm trying something new. But don't worry. I'll include plenty of my standard dragonflies and damselflies with each shipment. I still do those by hand. These are my Maiden series."

She set out two more cards. In one, a serious-faced woman held a dazzling yellow-and-orange sun in front of her chest. Her heart radiated light. In the other, a woman in a long, white tunic reclined on a boulder beside dark blue water. Behind her, emerald ferns and deep green trees gave the scene a fairy glen feel. A damselfly perched on the boulder beside the woman's foot.

"They're beautiful."

Mom lowered her shoulders. "I'm so glad you like them."

Half an hour must have passed before I got up the courage to ask, "How do you do it every day?"

"Do what?"

"Work up here, surrounded by all these memories."

Tears crested her eyes. Mom brushed them away with the paint-stained sleeve of her sweatshirt. "I lit a tea candle every morning. I told myself I had to work and could not fall apart until the candle guttered."

"Did it work?"

She shook her head. "Not at first. But I had to support us, so I kept trying. Finally, I made it."

"Wow."

"Working in the studio was easy compared to going into our bedroom every night." Mom sighed. "I can't believe it's been almost a year."

"Yeah. Halloween is *so* not my favorite holiday anymore."

Mom arched her brows. "Mine either."

I glanced at the three easels set up near the windows. "The collages look great."

Mom's expression brightened. "I have an appointment with a gallery next week."

"Awesome!"

"I talked to your father while I was working on them."

"Was he calling from a satellite phone in heaven?"

Mom bumped her shoulder against mine. "No, but he would if he could."

"He'd be too busy doing a photo essay on Gandhi or something."

"From war to peace. That would be a nice change." Mom sighed. "Anyway, I tell him about you. How you dyed your hair, that you wear his cap. Those sorts of things."

I swallowed the enormous lump lodged in my throat. "Sarah says the veil between worlds is thin this time of year."

Mom twisted her emerald wedding ring. "I know. The house feels different, like there's something going on we can't quite see."

I debated telling her about *Teen Wytche.*

"How is Parvani coming along with her witchcraft project?"

I blanked, but then remembered the little lie I had told her in the bookstore. "I don't know."

"Madrun Ravenwood has her eye on Parvani. Any idea why?"

I shrugged, which technically wasn't lying. I slid another card into an envelope.

"Parvani doesn't seem like the type to dabble in the Craft, unless she was desperate."

"What do you mean?"

"Well, say she decided to do a spell to help her maintain her A average."

"She wouldn't be harming anyone if she did," I said, thinking of my spell for help in math and science.

"Maybe not, but what if she believed magick could help her become a ballerina again? She might hurt herself."

Wait a minute. "Sounds like you know a lot about the Craft."

"I studied it out of self-defense."

"Why?"

"I went to school with Madrun Ravenwood, remember? And we both had a crush on your dad."

My heart skipped several beats. "You didn't do anything to bind Dad to you, did you?"

Mom remained silent. My pulse spiked. "I was tempted," she said at last. "Especially since I thought Madrun was up to something. But now I'm so glad I didn't."

"Why?"

Mom's eyes welled, making me sorry I had asked. "Because if I had, I would never have been sure he loved me. I'd always fear he had run off to dangerous countries to escape me."

I clasped her arm. "That's not why he did it."

She patted my hand. "I know." Her voice sounded choked. I knew, spell or no spell, Mom harbored the same fear I did — Dad hadn't loved us enough to stay home.

"Your Nana dabbles in the Craft." Mom sniffed. "She must not be any good."

"Why do you say that?"

"Because she promised to put a protection spell around Dash."

"Are you serious?"

Mom's lower lip quivered.

"You can't blame Nana for Dad's death." *It's my fault, not hers. He gave me his lucky cap.*

Mom shrugged and arched her eyebrows, like she didn't believe me. Then she cleared her throat, a sure sign she intended to change the subject. "It's nice to see you and Jordan getting along again."

"Yeah." I reached for a second batch of cards and glanced at the clock. Eleven-fifteen. In an hour, I could try to call Parvani. With any luck she'd be in Mr. Ross's room, or the library, and miss the gossip hotline.

Mom slid one of the water maidens into an envelope. "Isn't it weird? You and Jordan have hardly spoken to each other in years, and now you're buddies again."

I did not want to discuss Jordan with Mom, so I reached for another card.

"Your dad always hoped you and Jordan would become friends again. Maybe he's helping you along."

"Sure, Mom. Dad's playing cupid from the great beyond."

"Stranger things have happened."

I thought of *Teen Wytche* transforming into a real grimoire. What if Dad had guided me to the spell book?

CHAPTER TWENTY-ONE

Mom didn't break for lunch until one, so I missed my chance to call Parvani. Then, before I knew it, three forty-five had arrived. I paced my room, picking my way around the piles of clothes that had mushroomed again. Twice I reached for the phone, then talked myself out of it.

By four o'clock I started to wonder — did Parvani have piano today? Math club? Community service? Why hadn't she called? Was she still speaking to me? Had Salem warned her not to do the spell?

I reached for my cell. It rang as I touched it, nearly giving me a heart attack. "Hello?"

"Zhù is missing again." Parvani sounded breathless.

"What?"

"I happened to be passing by Room 222 when sixth period got out. No Zhù. Then after school, I ran into someone who has seventh period Spanish. She said Zhù didn't make it to Spanish either."

"Maybe he's out sick."

"He was in HG before lunch," Parvani reported. I heard the rustle of satin and figured she had just sat down on her canopy bed. The pink duvet matched Parvani's old toe shoes. She'd gone through tons of pairs before she'd had to give up ballet. They were tacked up on her walls, creating a three-dimensional border along the top. The effect was way cool, though kind of sad, given how much Parvani missed performing.

"Have you tried texting him?"

"Yeah. No response. Maybe he is blocking my number."

"Zhù wouldn't do that. He's crazy about you."

"Get serious." Parvani's voice softened like she wanted to believe me.

"I am serious. You're the only one who can't see it."

"We're just friends."

Yeah, like Jordan and me. I heard more satin rustling.

"Evie, you still there?"

"I'm here. Listen. Don't worry. I bet you'll hear from Zhù by tea time."

Parvani sighed. I could just imagine her adjusting her glasses. "All right. But let me give you his number. Maybe you could try calling him."

"And say what?"

"Make up something about Yearbook. I don't know." She proceeded to give me Zhù's cell phone number. I wrote it down in pencil on the back of an old movie ticket stub. "How was your first day of suspension?"

"Okay. Mom's on deadline, so she made me stuff envelopes all day."

"Oh, fun. Well, I better do my homework before the Terrors get back from karate."

"Okay. About the spell…"

The line went dead.

Parvani hadn't mentioned Jordan. Not once. Which made me wonder — what if I could get Zhù to ask Parvani to the

Halloween dance? Thinking of our tutoring date on Saturday, I decided to go online and check my homework assignments on the school's website. I didn't want him to cancel on me because I had missed class, too.

The homework for Spanish involved reviewing what we had studied earlier in the week, so my two-day suspension shouldn't disqualify me as a tutor. Operation Get-Zhù-To-Sweep-Parvani-Off-Her-Feet could commence.

I waited until I had finished the homework and eaten dinner before I called Zhù. After the fifth ring, I heard, "Hey. You've reached the Zhù-man's voicemail. You know what to do."

Zhù-man? I tried not to laugh. "*Hola* Zhù-man. It's Evie. Just confirming I'm still on top of Spanish, despite my two-day house arrest. So see you Saturday at four. *Adiós.*" *At least now if Parvani asks, I can say I called Zhù. I just can't tell her why.*

Zhù didn't call back in the evening, or the next day. By Saturday, I started to worry. Maybe he did have a dread disease. Or maybe his parents had taken away his phone. Then again, it was hard to imagine Zhù going over his allotted minutes.

That afternoon, an hour before we were supposed to meet, I was deep into studying *Teen Wytche,* wearing the pentacle necklace hidden beneath my shirt. My phone rang. "Hello?"

"Evie, it's Zhù."

I sat up straighter in the beanbag chair. "Hey. What's up? Are you still coming over?"

"Yeah." His voice sounded funny, like he was running or something. Then I heard a small thud. "I just wanted to make sure you'd be home. Sorry I didn't get back to you sooner." His voice caught again, and I heard another light thud.

"What are you doing?"

"What? Oh, just jumping over some stuff my sister left out. Your house at four?"

"Sure."

"Great. Thanks."

I pushed up Dad's cap and scratched my head.

***

An hour later, the doorbell rang. Mom got to the front door before me and greeted Zhù. She waved to his mother, who sat behind the wheel of a blue, older-model BMW. A stiff autumn breeze blew red and yellow maple leaves across the driveway as Mrs. Wong drove off.

Zhù's hair was wet and shiny and he smelled yummy, like he had just gotten out of the shower. He wore jeans and a crimson Stanford sweatshirt. I wore jeans and my navy Cal hoodie. *This does not bode well.* The two schools were bitter rivals.

Since there was no Plan B, I forged ahead. "Come in out of the wind," I said. Mom opened the door wider so Zhù could enter. I held Baby by the collar. *"Hola."*

"Hola."

Mom closed the door behind him. "I'll be in my bedroom if you need anything." She wore a blissful expression, as she always did after a shipment of cards went out on time. I figured she'd spend the next two days immersed in a romance novel.

"Okay. Thanks." I led Zhù into the kitchen.

His chest puffed out as he inhaled the warm scent of baked chocolate goodness. Just as I'd hoped, he eyed the pan of steaming brownies. I'd babysat enough times to know how to woo kids — how much harder could it be to bend a male math geek to my will? Judging from Zhù's hopeful expression as he laid his backpack on the kitchen table, the answer was, not too hard.

"Would you like a brownie?"

"Sí. Gracias." Zhù pulled out a chair and sat down. His back stayed board-straight, not touching the chair, the same perfect posture as Parvani.

I placed three brownies on a plate for him. *Teen Wytche* said three, seven, nine, and twenty-one are lucky numbers. He inhaled two before I could even open my textbook. "I didn't have time to eat after my workout," Zhù explained.

"Would you like some water or milk? Hot apple cider?" Mom doesn't allow soda in the house, so his options were kind of limited.

"Water, please."

"Sure." Since I was already ruining my appetite for dinner, I threw a bag of popcorn in the microwave. Popping sounds filled the kitchen, and the theater-like odor of butter and salt overlaid the rich chocolate scent. At Zhù's feet, Baby salivated.

I handed Zhù tall tumblers of water for both of us, and then poured the popcorn into the blue snowman bowl. "Have you read the vocabulary list?" I asked.

A few kernels spilled out of Zhù's hand and left grease marks on his binder paper. "No. I haven't had time to check online yet."

He did look kind of tired, in an otherwise-fit way. "Here. I made you a copy."

"Thanks."

We reviewed pronunciation and memorized which way the accent marks should slant. Then we moved on to expressions. I was so going to earn my ten dollars an hour.

"Me gusta béisbol. I like baseball," Zhù said.

"Bueno." I decided to sneak in a reference to Parvani. *"Parvani gusta escuchar música."*

"I know. Sometimes we share her ear buds."

"Her list is a little heavy on classical. Probably because she plays piano, and used to dance ballet."

"Yeah. Me too." He stared down at my notes.

I was pretty sure he just meant he liked classical music, but maybe he played piano as well. I'd heard music and math used the same part of the brain, which may have been why I couldn't do either. "Of course, she also likes a lot of modern stuff," I added. "You know, stuff you can dance to." *Hint. Hint.*

Zhù bit into his third brownie and nodded.

"You know, she's been worried about you."

He stopped mid-chew. "No way. Why?"

"Because you keep missing your afternoon classes. She's afraid you might have a dread disease."

Zhù resumed chewing. And blinking. For a smart guy, he sure appeared dumbfounded. "I'm surprised she noticed."

"Oh, she noticed." *And she'd kill me if she knew I said anything.*

A long moment of silence descended. I hoped Zhù would tell me why he'd been absent. Instead, he grabbed a handful of popcorn and studied my notes. I gave up and spent the next hour sprinkling in Parvani's name as much as I could without seeming too obvious. I swore I could see Zhù taking mental notes. He must have kept a huge file in his head marked *Parvani.*

"You two sure have a lot in common," I said as our time ended.

He blinked at me from behind those rimless John Lennon glasses. "Yeah. Too bad *opposites* attract."

"Not always. Besides, I hear that never lasts." At least I hoped it didn't, in Parvani's case.

The doorbell rang, setting off gruff barking from Baby. "Must be my mother." He handed me a ten and a five. "We went over a little."

"You don't have to pay me extra," I protested.

"I want to. Thanks for all the help. Same time next week?" The bell rang again. Mom must have been in the bathroom, or immersed in her novel. I opened the door. "Parvani!"

"Hey." Her triumphant expression dissolved when she noticed Zhù standing behind me. Her head jerked, as if her world had upended. "Zhù! What are you doing here?"

Zhù and I gaped at each other, trying to come up with a plausible explanation.

"Yearbook," I blurted out.

Zhù exhaled a long, raspy breath. The boy sucked at acting.

Parvani's perfect brows stitched together, as if we were an algebra equation where x didn't quite equal two. Which happens to me a lot, but not to Parvani. Her nostrils flared. I had the terrible feeling popcorn and brownie smells clung to us. I checked the front of my sweatshirt for crumbs.

"Wouldn't a phone call have been easier?" Parvani asked, her voice cold.

"Um." Well, she had us there.

Zhù fished a turquoise flash drive out of his backpack. "You should make a copy of this." He handed the device to me. "It has all the photos we worked on."

"Oh, right." *Quick thinking.* I slipped the flash drive into my pocket. "Good thing you remembered. We could do it now…"

Over the almost silent purr of Dr. Hyde-Smith's Lexus came the unmistakable sound of a skateboard rolling over blacktop. The rhythmic noise grew louder. Jordan maneuvered into view, eddies of wind-tossed leaves swirling at his feet.

Jordan jumped the curb. For a split second he sailed in silence, then slapped down hard. The wheels rolled across the concrete, sounding coarse and gritty. Then he picked up speed, skating full out, and shredded the air, going higher than I had ever seen. I held my breath until he landed safely on the driveway. He slowed to a stop and stomped on the back tip of his board. The front end catapulted into his hand.

Zhù stiffened. Parvani blinked several times. My insides did a quick rollercoaster dive.

"Hey." Jordan knuckle bumped Zhù, then flashed an ingratiating grin at Parvani and me. Unbuckling his helmet, he glanced down at the small bag Parvani held in a white-knuckled grip. "Someone's birthday?"

"No." Parvani glanced at her dad. He gestured for her to hurry up.

"Actually," Parvani said in her most clipped British way, "I wanted to show Evie something."

I peeked at the bag and recognized Sage Mage's blue tissue paper and the lingering stench of incense. "But since you have company," Parvani continued in a strangled voice, "it can wait."

"What did you procure?" Zhù asked.

"A Buddha statue."

"Cool," Jordan said.

Parvani adjusted her glasses. "I want to pick up the stuff I left here the other day." Icy fury and wasp-like determination laced her voice. She pushed between Zhù and me.

"I'll be right back." I threw Zhù a pleading glance, then flew back to my room. Parvani knelt on the floor, stuffing the black handled knife and the pink candle into the bag with the river rocks.

"You told me to check on Zhù. Why are you mad?"

"I told you to call him, not date him."

"This wasn't a date!"

"I thought I could trust you."

"You can. I have no interest in Zhù." *Just Jordan.*

"Right." Parvani peered under my math book and some papers on my desk. "Where's *Teen Wytche?*"

"We need to talk. The book says there are serious repercussions if you direct a love spell at a particular person."

"Is that why you directed your spell at two people?" She picked up a dirty blouse and a pair of mud-stained jeans, unearthing the spell book. At least she hadn't noticed the willow wand.

"What are you talking about?"

"You know what I mean. Zhù and Jordan."

"Are you crazy? I didn't perform a love spell on either of them."

A knock on my bedroom door silenced us. I turned my back on Parvani and opened it.

"Hey," Jordan said. "Parvani, your dad looks like he's going to have a fit or something. You better get out there."

"He can wait another minute. He and my mother are headed off on one of their little vacations from the kids."

That might partially explain why she's so mad.

Jordan stepped back so Parvani could storm past. He glanced up at my Shay Stewart shrine and his eyebrows bounced toward his shaggy bangs.

With humiliation blazing across my cheeks, I ran after Parvani.

"I expected more from you," Parvani scolded Zhù. Her voice cracked as she shouldered past him.

"Parvani..." Zhù reached out, but she shrugged him off. Bent beneath the weighty magical objects, she speed-walked to the Lexus. She climbed into the cream-colored interior, closed the door, and didn't look back.

Behind me, the cracked entry tile made a wretched scraping sound. "Did I miss something?"

I shook my head and breathed in the lingering odor of incense. Realization sucker-punched me. *Buddha.* Parvani had her god figure. If she got her hands on a goddess, a wand, and a pentacle, she could perform the spell. She'd be unstoppable.

Jordan stood so close behind me I could feel the heat radiating from his body. I inhaled his outdoorsy scent, longing to wrap my arms around him and keep him from slipping away again.

CHAPTER
TWENTY-TWO

Dad had told me about men and women he'd seen in war —
normal, decent human beings who'd cracked under the pressure.
Like soldiers on recon that stayed too long in a window, when they
should have ducked. He told me how being under fire changes
you, erodes your soul.

I wondered about Parvani's pressure to get straight A's. All
the activities designed to help her either get into a top college or
forget about ballet. And there was Jordan, seemingly filled with
ease, a commodity Parvani desperately needed and longed for.

Zhù drove off with his dad. Jordan headed for the kitchen.
I hung back, my mind on Parvani. *We're best friends. She should
know I'd never steal from her, even if I did think she was trying to
take Jordan from me.*

"Can I have a brownie?" Jordan called out.

"Sure." I hustled after him. *Forget sneaking makeup. I should
just walk around with a plate of chocolate.*

Baby trotted ahead of me and made a beeline for the floor
beneath the kitchen table. Snuffling like a pig hunting truffles,
she tracked down a couple of popcorn kernels. Jordan glanced at
the table littered with Spanish worksheets and notes. He blinked

a couple of times, taking in the incriminating popcorn bowl and the two water glasses.

"Are you and Zhù study partners?" He sounded surprised, and kind of hurt.

This is why I hate to lie. One always leads to another.

I handed Jordan a brownie. "I was working on Spanish when Zhù stopped by to go over some stuff for Yearbook. Our first set of pages is due on Wednesday."

"Oh." Jordan sounded relieved. "Which reminds me." He polished off the brownie in two giant bites then slid his backpack off his shoulder and unzipped it. He pulled out a folder marked *Biology*. He had drawn a skateboarder flying over the L. "We have a lab report due on Monday."

I groaned.

"The good news is you missed yesterday's quiz."

"Which I'll have to make up at lunch on Monday, along with the quiz I missed in math." *Don't my teachers realize I have karmic issues to deal with?*

"Don't worry. I'll help you. There's no football practice tomorrow, so I'll come over after I take Grandpa to the VFW breakfast."

The knot of fear in my stomach loosened several notches. I poured him a glass of milk. "Awesome. Thanks."

He handed me a worksheet. "Here's our next assignment. We're supposed to create a population growth model and predict the outcome."

I predict Parvani will do the love spell and ruin all our lives.

Jordan downed half the milk. "Are you burned out? We can wait until tomorrow."

"No, let's get it over with. Just give me a sec to clean up." I stacked the Spanish notes and textbook together and moved them to the desk, and then cleared away the popcorn bowl and Zhù's glass. I unearthed my Bio book, which weighed over five pounds, and thudded it onto the table.

"Okay, I'm ready." I sat down and reached for my water. "What do we need to do?"

"Make lots of babies."

I had just taken a sip of water and nearly spit on him, covering my mouth just in time. Liquid dripped down my chin as a blush flamed my cheeks.

Jordan laughed. "Got you."

I grabbed a napkin to sop up the mess then threw it at him. Jordan deflected the wet missile with a well-timed swat. *Athletes.* Still, it was nice to see him smile.

"Rabbit babies," Jordan explained, his lake-blue eyes twinkling. "It seems," he studied the worksheet for a moment, "two rabbits got swept out to sea, but managed to scramble up onto a piece of driftwood. It carried them to an island."

"I suppose we're talking about a female and a male rabbit?"

"You know, it doesn't say," Jordan replied.

"Well, it says they mated and started reproducing, so let's assume Max and Charlotte were of the correct genders."

"Max and Charlotte?"

"Charlotte is not the type of girl to mate with just anyone. She and Max had been dating for years before the storm caught them."

Jordan just stared at me for a second, then his lips lifted into a sly grin. "Max and Charlotte declared themselves captains of their driftwood boat and married each other before landing on the island."

"Good thing." I imagined writing Mr. and Mrs. Kent around the holes in my binder paper. "Otherwise, they would have had to practice abstinence when they got to the island."

"Causing us to flunk this assignment."

"We wouldn't want that," I said.

"No."

I was so not thinking about Biology anymore. Well, not rabbit biology.

"Max and Charlotte had plenty of food and no predators on the island." Jordan brought me back to reality. "So what type of growth would we expect?"

I remembered this part. "Exponential growth."

Jordan's pencil scratched across the worksheet as he wrote down my answer. "And what equation describes this growth?"

I knew he knew the answer. The question was, did I? "$G=rN$?"

Jordan beamed. "See, you know this stuff."

I wanted to take our picture, freeze the moment. But I noticed the next part of the project involved calculating and graphing. Time to stall. "What do you think about Parvani?"

Jordan shrugged. "I dunno. She's nice, I guess. I feel sorry for her."

"She's one of the richest kids at school. Why do you feel sorry for her?"

Jordan placed his pencil on top of the worksheet and stretched. "One time, in English, we had to read aloud from our journal. Parvani had written about how she used to get up at five in the morning to take ballet lessons. Then after school, she rehearsed for another hour."

I nodded.

"Can you believe it?" Jordan said. "Even though she was kind of young, her teachers, like, decided she could go *en pointe.*"

"I've seen her old toe shoes."

"Then one day, wham! A stress fracture."

"I know. She tried to hide it, which made things worse, and now she can't dance anymore."

"It made me think," Jordan continued. "What if something similar happened to me and I had to bail on skateboarding?"

"I bet your parents would enroll you in a bunch of other stuff to keep your mind off what you had lost."

"As if I could forget. In a way, you're luckier than Parvani. At least there's a chance you'll be able to take photos again."

What if Parvani thinks I should just snap out of it? Maybe she thinks I'm the one who has everything — including both of the guys she likes, and the ability to pursue my passion.

"Ready to calculate the approximate growth in Charlotte and Max's brood?" Jordan asked.

I wasn't sure about calculating the intrinsic rate of increase for rabbits. But I had a pretty clear hypothesis about my chances of stopping Parvani from casting the love spell.

Zero.

CHAPTER TWENTY-THREE

After Jordan left, Mom and I made turkey tacos. Mom must have seen the frantic, distracted look in my eyes, because for once she didn't make me do the dishes. Maybe I had reaped good karma for helping her with the greeting cards.

Free from indentured servitude, I rushed to my room and searched for Parvani's list of things we needed for a circle. I had just discovered it under my bed when the phone rang. Seeing Salem's name on the caller ID, I grabbed it before Mom could pick it up in the kitchen.

"Hello?"

"Hi Evie, it's Sarah."

"Where are you?" I shivered. Mom hadn't kicked on the heater yet. "You sound far away."

"Massachusetts. I'm on my cell. We left in a hurry, and I forgot my charger. So we'll have to talk fast before I run out of battery."

"Why are you in Massachusetts?"

"My sister had a breakdown. My parents didn't know who to leave me with, so we all flew out to check on Amy."

"Is she okay?"

"No. Being perfect was harder on her than anyone realized. We brought Einstein. Pets are good therapy."

"If your parents need to stay there, we'll take you in. Mom won't mind."

"Gee, thanks. I'll tell my parents. What's happening with you and Parvani?"

"She's furious with me and I'm worried she'll perform the spell." I recited the abridged version, leaving out the part about tutoring Zhù.

"We have one hope," Salem declared. "You said Parvani is thorough, right?"

"True."

"Then she'll read the warnings, and she won't direct the spell at Jordan."

"What if she doesn't read any further than the optimal time frame? The full moon is tonight."

"Then we might have a problem. Does she have everything she needs to cast a circle?"

I scanned the list. My heart sprinted. "I'm wearing your necklace. She doesn't have a pentacle."

"Maybe she won't realize she can just draw one."

"She doesn't have a goddess figure."

"I bet there's a silver candlestick somewhere in her mansion."

"Will that work?" I asked.

"Sure, as long as she puts a white candle in it."

"Her parents throw lots of parties. They have tons of white candles." A new thought hit me. "Parvani's parents are out of town. The housekeeper will be in charge, and she'll have her hands full with the twins."

"You're doomed." The dying battery garbled the rest of her words.

"Is there a counter spell?" I shouted over the static.

Salem's voice cut off.

Frantic, I dialed Parvani's number. No answer. She'd probably checked the caller ID and refused to pick up. Now what? Should I ask Mom to drive me over there and help me storm Parvani's gate?

I went to the living room and slipped out the sliding glass door. A crisp wind sluiced through the birch trees and the Japanese maple, ringing a dragon-shaped metal wind chime. I hugged my arms to my torso and walked to the edge of the concrete patio. A bat swooped near my head, then flew off.

A fine mist dampened my cheeks as I scanned the night sky. The moon, half hidden by the clouds, appeared full, potent, and ripe for fueling a love spell. It would make a great photo if I used Dad's old Nikon with the right lens.

An owl *hoo-hooed* from the trees, and something small and quick rustled through the ivy. Spooked, I hurried back indoors. I tried Parvani's number again. This time when she didn't answer, I pictured her highlighting, or gathering magical objects. Or worse, spell casting.

Chilled, I slipped my hands into my sweatshirt pocket. My fingers bumped against Zhù's flash drive. I headed for the computer, determined to control what I could, or at least to take my mind off Parvani for a while.

One computer was in the studio, the other on the desk in the kitchen. I decided to head for the latter. Mom believed computers should be in public areas so she could snoop over my shoulder. You know, in case I underwent a personality change and started surfing porn sites or taking up with predators disguised as wannabe friends. *Like I'm naive enough to put private information or my picture on a social network site, or leave my page set to public.*

Mom peeled off yellow dishwashing gloves. "Hey, sweetie. What are you up to?"

I pressed the power button on the computer. The start-up chord sounded and the monitor went sky blue. "Zhù brought over the edits he did for Yearbook. I thought I'd check them out before bed."

"He seems like a good kid." Mom picked up a dishtowel and started to dry the dishes. The frying pan clattered as she put it away. She moved on to the glass brownie pan.

I switched into photo editor mode. Rows of photos the size of postage stamps appeared on the computer screen. The shots I had taken of the drama club drew my attention. I clicked on a close-up of Pilar and Nazario.

"Wow," Mom said over my shoulder.

"I took it at the dress rehearsal for *Of Mice and Men*."

"*You* took the picture?"

"Yep. The same day I broke Evan's foot." I lifted Dad's cap and pushed my fingers through my hair. "Zhù did a good job cropping it."

Mom squeezed my shoulders. "He had a great photo to work with." She dragged a chair to the desk and plopped down beside me. We examined the series I had taken. "Incredible," Mom said. "Are there more?"

"There should be. Hang on." I clicked on the blue side bar and slid to the top of the page. I didn't recognize the first row of pictures.

"Are those from school?" Mom asked.

"I don't think so. It doesn't look like the auditorium." I clicked on the first photo and enlarged it. A shot popped up of dancers in leotards.

Mom leaned forward. "It looks like a ballet rehearsal." She skimmed her finger above the surface of the monitor, reading the dancers faces as if they were dots of Braille. She paused. "Is that Zhù?"

I removed Dad's cap and studied the photo. Same short ebony hair, rimless glasses, sculpted cheekbones, familiar humorless concentration, and — whoa — a skin-tight, sleeveless tee and impressive biceps? My gaze dropped to navy running shorts, muscular legs, and ballet shoes.

Crap...Zhù's gay.

CHAPTER TWENTY-FOUR

My brain felt microwaved. Zhù had been my last hope. I had no Plan B. The tacos churned inside my stomach. I grasped for a logical explanation. "Maybe Zhù took up ballet to impress Parvani?"

"I doubt it." Mom swiped the drying cloth across the plastic tongs we had used to flip the tortillas. "Ballet takes real dedication. Think of how many hours you have to practice. You don't do it for someone else."

"Yeah. Especially knowing what homophobic jerks like the Smash Heads would do if they found out."

"Being a dancer doesn't mean for certain he's gay. You said he has a crush on Parvani."

"He sure acts likes he does."

My gay radar, or gaydar as Parvani calls it, wavered. I had always thought of Zhù as kind of a brainy goof — a *heterosexual* brainy goof. Had I been wrong all these years? I studied the picture again and sighed. *Guys just don't look straight in ballet shoes. Then again, how many straight guys get highlights?*

Mom pointed to a familiar-looking girl in the ensemble. "There's Zhù's sister, Ming. When I ran into Mrs. Wong at the grocery store last week, she mentioned Ming had won a role in the Nutcracker. Maybe Zhù did too."

"Then he must be good." Parvani would be impressed. *Zhù should tell her.* Maybe it would stop Parvani from ensnaring Jordan with a love spell.

I resolved to speed up Operation Get-Zhù-To-Sweep-Parvani-Off-Her-Feet. The plan might need to be tweaked. First, I'd have to convince Zhù to tell Parvani he had a major crush on her, or that he shared her passion for ballet. Or both.

The scheme might work, if Parvani hasn't already cast the spell.

***

By Sunday afternoon, I had transferred the yearbook photos onto a new flash drive and stashed it in my backpack. I kept checking the time. How late could the VFW breakfast last, anyway?

When Jordan didn't show by two-thirty, I worried something had happened. By three, I paced my room, convinced he had stood me up. He'd probably gone skateboarding.

I tamped down the rising tsunami of old hurt and pulled out Jordan's notes. It would have been nice to have him or Parvani to walk me through them, but no way would I call either of them. I was on my own.

Again.

Afterward, I ran through my mental worry list. Yearbook — done. Math — done enough. Parvani — who knew? What else? Oh yeah, Tommy Deitch.

Surely the Smash Heads' honor code required retaliation if one member got hurt and/or suspended. I did not want to be on Tommy's Kids-to-Demolish list. During the switch between classes, I could hide in the center of the throng. I'm average height. Only one thing would make me stand out — the camouflage hat.

I removed Dad's cap and ran my thumb over the stiff visor. Feeling like a traitor, or at least a coward, I unzipped my backpack and stuffed the cap in next to my Bio binder. With or without the hat, though, I'd be vulnerable crossing the wide-open field. And what about Capture the Flag?

I poked at the pile of clothes that had hidden *Teen Wytche.* Maybe the book contained a protection spell. Too bad I couldn't call Parvani and ask her to look it up. If Salem were around, she'd help. I decided to wing it. After all, the last spell I'd done had worked out pretty well.

Since Parvani had confiscated all the circle stuff, I improvised. Luckily, I still had my compass, which I placed in the middle of the floor. Remembering the quarters represented the four elements as well as the four directions, I began to search. A potted African violet from the bathroom would do for earth. A speckled shell that had been gathering dust on my windowsill for three years could represent water. A tea light for fire was a no-brainer. Air had me stumped. A feather?

Baby cocked her head toward the backyard. The dragon wind chime Dad had bought clanged in the wind. He used to say the metallic ring reminded him of our favorite kung fu movies. I ran out back and lifted the chime off its hook.

Back in my room, I added the troll and the tiara, and figured I was good to go. Now I just had to come up with a spell. Sinking into the beanbag chair, I closed my eyes. A line from the inner goddess article floated into my mind.

Envision what you'd like to experience.

"I'd like to be invisible to Tommy Deitch," I said out loud. Maybe I could create a Don't-See-Me spell.

Since Jordan's picture had fallen into the circle before, I figured photos had good mojo for me. I dug out last year's yearbook and scanned Tommy's picture into the computer. A few minutes later, I had isolated, enlarged, and printed Tommy's malevolent face. I hoped his vile image wouldn't crash the hard drive.

I had the strong sense neither Mom nor Salem would approve of my dabbling. Ignoring the strident warnings sounding in my head, I locked the bedroom door and cast the Don't-See-Me spell.

****

Monday morning, I woke sweaty and queasy. My best friend had probably done something we'd both regret. Tommy Deitch would be gunning for me. My permanent school record would be forever tainted by my suspension, and I no longer had any hope of getting into even a fourth-tier college. *And* I had to take two make-up tests involving math.

I might as well forget about signing up for sophomore classes next year. My fate is pretty much sealed.

Mom drove the carpool today. She didn't mention Dad's cap, though I know she noticed my bare head. My strawberry outgrowth clashing with my Intensely Autumn hair dye was hard to overlook. Before we left, I kept waiting for a call from Mrs. Hyde-Smith saying she'd be driving Parvani today. Then I remembered Parvani's parents were in the wine country. No way would the housekeeper risk trouble by letting Parvani stay home. We'd be stuck with each other.

Just in case Parvani had done the right thing and decided not to perform the spell, I sat in the back seat of the Volvo, ready to be friends again. When we reached the Tudor mansion, Parvani strode toward the car without making eye contact, pulled open the front, passenger side door and sat in the front seat.

My jaw dropped.

"Good morning." Mom sounded a little surprised.

"Good morning," Parvani replied. No glance over her shoulder or, "Hey, Evie," or "Welcome back, Evie." No, "Sorry I was such a jerk on Saturday." *Nada.*

A yellow maple leaf larger than my hand flew onto the windshield and stuck. The silence grew so oppressive, Mom switched on the radio as soon as we rolled through the ornate wrought iron gate. When we reached school, Parvani lobbed a, "Thanks, Mrs. O'Reilly," over her shoulder, then struck out across the field alone.

Mom glanced over her shoulder. "Have a good one, sweetie."

"Yeah, right." I got out and scanned the field. No sign of Tommy. No sign of Jordan or Zhù, either. Feeling vulnerable without Dad's cap, I took a deep breath. I was going in.

I made it across the field and within sight of English before I spied Tommy. As he scanned the hall, his brown ADD eyes lit up like forbidden Fourth of July fireworks. Two freshmen scurried out of his way, leaving just Tommy and me. With nowhere to hide and my heart thudding like a Whack-A-Mole game, I reached for the topaz in my front jeans pocket.

Tommy got within five feet of me and showed no sign of seeing me or slowing down. I couldn't tell if he was playing a pedestrian version of chicken or if, by magic, he didn't know I was there. He plowed closer and I could smell the cola and chocolate cereal on his breath.

Bam! One second Tommy towered before me, and the next second he flew sideways. "Watch where you're going, jerk."

"Wow. Sorry, man." Zhù readjusted his backpack and tossed me a look. I slid over next to him, putting more distance between Tommy and me.

Tommy rubbed his arm. "Make sure it doesn't happen again." He glared at Zhù then stalked off, never once glancing my way.

"Wow, Evie. He acted like he didn't even see you."

"I know." *The spell worked!* My eyes felt as round as my troll doll's. "Zhù, did you crash him on purpose?"

"Of course not." He pushed his rimless glasses up the bridge of his nose. "Jefferson High School does not condone violence. Too bad for Tommy I'm such a klutz."

"Yeah, right." We fell into step together. "I'm not looking forward to Evan's return."

Zhù shrugged. "He'll be on crutches. We'll hear him coming."

I had to smile. No wonder Parvani liked Zhù so much. "Well, you're my hero." I leaned close and whispered, "I went through the pictures on the flash drive you gave me. Some of them weren't from school."

Confusion leapt like a *grand jeté* across Zhù's face. He halted as realization and panic dawned in his eyes. "Evie..."

"Don't worry. I copied the yearbook pictures onto this." I pulled out a pink flash drive from the outer pocket of my backpack. "Yours is at my house where no one will see it. You can pick it up whenever you want."

"You didn't tell anyone?"

"Of course not. My mother was sitting next to me, but she won't tell anyone."

We walked past a bulletin board covered in bright orange posters for the Halloween dance competing with green Go Wildcats placards. I gritted my teeth. Just what I needed — reminders of a dance Jordan would probably attend with Parvani.

"The whole ballet thing started as a fluke," Zhù explained. "My mother would pick Ming and me up from school, then I'd have to hang out until Ming finished her ballet lesson. I got bored, so one day I tried out."

"Then you're not gay? I mean, I never thought you were. I thought you had a crush on Parvani. Personally, I don't care if you're gay…"

"Evie." Zhù clasped my shoulders. "I'm not gay."

I tried to mask my relief. Operation Get-Zhù-To Sweep-Parvani-Off-Her-Feet was back on. "Did you audition for the Nutcracker?"

He beamed. "Two parts. Drosselmeyer's nephew and…"

The bell blared. "We're going to be tardy." I pocketed the flash drive, said a quick, "Bye," and sprinted for English.

"Be careful in gym," Zhù called out.

"Don't worry," I said in my best I've-got-it-covered voice. But I didn't have it covered. Fear gnawed my guts. If it didn't let up soon, I'd be spending gym in the girl's bathroom.

At least there I'd be safe from Tommy.

CHAPTER
TWENTY-FIVE

"Deitch, red team." Coach Willis jerked his thumb in my general direction.

My scarlet armband constricted like a tourniquet. I searched again for Jordan, my shoulders hunched against the wind. It was upsetting enough he had gone AWOL on me yesterday, but today? With Parvani on the yellow team, I had no friends, just hostiles, on both sides of the orange cones. *Great. Just great.*

Tommy strode into red territory, slamming shoulders with any kid who didn't step aside quickly enough. I pulled the topaz from my pocket and clutched it.

Tommy didn't seem to notice me. I figured he wasn't smart enough for subterfuge, but just in case, I positioned myself as far from him as possible. Staying within Coach Willis's eyesight, I hugged the sideline, halfway between the front line attackers and Tommy.

Across the divide, Parvani did a nervous side-to-side ballet leap. Was it my imagination, or did she appear guilty and full of regret? She flicked her fingers, releasing tension. Was she planning a suicide run? Had she gone insane?

Had she performed the love spell?

A row of birch and liquid amber trees shielded the football field from the road. An erratic wind pushed through them, knocking foliage from the branches. Leaves swooped between players, grazing heads and landing on shoulders. Without Dad's cap, the wind whipped my hair across my face, stinging my eyes and cheeks.

I glanced back at Tommy. His elbows were bent, his hands fisted. His gaze appeared fixed on the opposite team's front line.

Relief rushed my veins. I leaned over, my hands propped against my thighs. Head up, I steeled myself for the whistle blast. When it pierced my eardrums, I didn't scream or jump. Instead, I squinted into the wind and trained my gaze on Tommy.

Tommy surged forward. Wearing a down vest like a flak jacket, he seemed impervious to the cold and sluicing wind. He kept thrusting out his arms, using his meaty hands to shove teammates out of the way.

"Go straight. Don't veer," I murmured like Subliminal Woman. "You don't see me."

Someone yelled, "O'Reilly, watch out!"

Two boys from the yellow team raced toward me, arms outstretched, ready to tag. I had nowhere to go but toward Tommy. Instinct took over, and before the warning voice inside my head could scream, "Let them tag you!", my legs started pumping.

A flash of long black hair appeared in my peripheral vision. Parvani. The rest of the yellow team's front line had abandoned her. The rising gale whipped her hair into Medusa-like dreadlocks. She must have moved wrong or been tagged hard. Something had happened, maybe to her old ballet injury, because she suddenly dropped and clutched her calf.

Adrenalin pounded my ears. I dodged a blonde wearing a yellow armband. The front line loomed ahead. I glanced back to get a fix on Tommy. He loved nothing better than easy prey, and there was Parvani, locked in his sights.

I sprinted through the melee, zigzagging like a Cal quarterback dodging the Stanford defense. The icy menace of Tommy's stare sliced through me and wrapped around Parvani.

Oh no. The Don't-See-Me spell.

Tommy charged like a crazed bull. The wet grass between us disappeared as he barreled closer and closer. Time shuddered to a stop. I tried to turn away but couldn't move. Shouts filled my ears. I couldn't understand them. My gaze had locked on the whites of Tommy's eyes.

I raised my arms to ward off the blow. The topaz flew from my hand. Whatever hope I'd had freefell. Two feet away. The stench of Tommy's sweat assaulted my nose. One foot.

Spell be done! I screamed inside my head.

A *zing* sliced the air.

Six inches.

Tommy's eyes widened.

The spell broke too late for him to stop.

Blackness. I had a vague sense of blindly flying backward. Then came the second impact, as unyielding as the first. The back of my head hit something hard. My forehead throbbed, as if my brain had slammed into it. White bursts punctuated the darkness.

I entered a cold, silent void. Then, as if someone had flipped a switch, a cosmic-sized monitor lit. It was like staring through a thick glass window where white, tormented forms sailed past in an endless loop. I *so* did not want to join them.

A tunnel of light appeared. Movies and television don't do it justice. It radiated pure love and light. More than anything I wanted to walk into it and bathe in its golden glory. I sensed

Dad's presence within the tunnel, but he didn't beckon to me. Crushed, I felt alone and abandoned. *Again.*

New images appeared before me — Jordan skateboarded past, all ease and grace, but a tear slid down his cheek and his nose was red. Parvani's eyes were filled with remorse. Mascara coursed down Salem's pale cheeks. The Zhù-man appeared lost, as if he were wearing pants without pockets and didn't know where to put his hands.

Sad-eyed Baby. Mom, her face grief-stricken.

Reluctantly, I slipped away from Dad and the beautiful golden light.

Someone shook me. I wanted to tell them to stop. My head hurt. My brain couldn't quite sequence the words in the right order.

"Evie. Can you hear me?" Coach Willis sounded far away, yet his breath warmed my face. It was hard to think with all the noise after the silence of the void.

More shaking.

I tried to open my eyes. They rolled beneath my closed lids, side to side, like I was speed-reading. A cool breeze slid over me, clearing some of the fuzz from my brain.

"Evie?" Parvani sounded worried, as if we were still friends.

"I'm telling you, I didn't see her."

Tommy.

"Yeah, because she was only *right in front of you.*" I'd never noticed before how much more British Parvani sounded when she was mad.

I willed my eyes to open. Blurry faces swam before me, whirling my stomach. Coach. Parvani. Beyond them, I saw a Tilt-O'-Whirl sea of anxious eyes and windswept hair. It would have made a cool photo if I could have gotten the shutter speed right.

I rolled over and threw up on Tommy's shoes. Several kids cried, "Eww!" and dodged out of the way. I wiped my mouth with the back of my hand, then flopped onto my back.

Coach asked, "How many fingers do you see?"

The vertigo made it difficult to tell. "Three? Four? No, two. Definitely two."

Coach and Parvani wore identical worried expressions.

"Don't make me count," I said. "I suck at math."

Parvani blinked behind her designer frames — her expression barely relaxed. Coach put a warm hand on my shoulder.

"Lie still." Coach pointed to one of the girls in the crowd and told her to run to the office, get the school nurse, and tell Mrs. Scroggins to call for an ambulance.

"Deitch, wipe off your shoes, then hightail it to the principal's office."

"But I tell you, I didn't see…"

"*Now*, Deitch." Coach removed his jacket and covered me from my shoulders to my hips.

My eyes fluttered closed.

"Stay with us Evie. Open your eyes."

CHAPTER TWENTY-SIX

I awoke to the disgusting taste of barf coating my mouth, the painful glare of fluorescent lights, and a monster headache.

Mom squeezed my hand. "How you feeling, sweetie?"

"I'm freezing. Where am I?"

"The emergency room." Mom took off her coat and draped it over the thin sheet covering me. She wore an olive turtleneck and jeans underneath. "You hit your head on a sprinkler. Luckily, it was a flat, plastic one. Took five stitches, though. You have a mild concussion."

I pulled her black wool coat up under my chin. The collar smelled of moisturizer and shampoo. "Anything to get out of taking a math quiz."

Mom snorted. "Tommy Deitch better get suspended."

"Mom…"

She got up and took a tissue from a dispenser on the counter. "I warned the school I'd sue them if they didn't protect you, and look where you ended up."

"Mom, don't sue!"

"If your dad were here…" She dabbed the tears streaming down her cheeks. The overhead fluorescents painted her in a harsh light, and I noticed the dark circles under her eyes.

"Mom. It's okay." I caught the hem of her top and pulled her closer. "I'm fine, except for the ringing in my ears and the pain in my head. Can we turn down the lights?"

"I'll check." She found a couple of switches near the striped privacy curtain and flicked off the light over the bed.

I tried to sit, which was a mondo mistake. Add dizziness and nausea to my list. "Can we leave?" I whined.

Someone whisked the plastic curtain aside with a ring of metal hooks sliding along the aluminum rail. A woman in aqua scrubs entered, holding a clipboard. "Anxious to go home, are you?"

I wondered if my brain was still misfiring, or if she actually sounded like Yoda. I shrugged, which sent pain darting up my sore shoulders.

"I'm Dr. Cameron. You must be Evie. My, we've had a run of students this week." Dr. Cameron flicked a pen light in my eyes, checked my blood pressure, and asked me all sorts of questions to determine if I had brain damage. Apparently I didn't, though I doubted the whole sprinkler scare would improve my math scores.

About three hours later, Dr. Cameron handed me a note excusing me from Gym for a week, and released me. "Keep a close eye on her for the next twenty-four hours," she warned Mom.

Great. As if Mom needs to be up all night making sure I don't slip into a coma.

When we got home, I checked the phone. No voicemails. I thought for sure Parvani would have called and left a message, but she hadn't. Obviously she didn't care I had ended up in the hospital. *You'd think she'd be worried, or at least grateful I stopped Tommy from pulverizing her.*

Maybe she was too busy checking on Jordan.

Not that I cared.

***

I spent Tuesday at home staring at the phone, which never rang. My mental worry meter buzzed all the way to Meltdown, thanks to the two make up quizzes I'd have to take on Wednesday. I worried about Jordan, and the possibility I didn't have a friend left in the world.

By Wednesday, the gash in the back of my head felt like someone had rammed a screwdriver into my skull. I considered playing the concussion card to eke out another sick day, but the pages were due in Yearbook, and thanks to Tommy I had yet to hand in the flash drive.

Mom arranged my hair into a short ponytail. "Did you cover up the stitches?" I asked.

"You can barely see them poking out," she promised.

I considered wearing Dad's cap, but figured it would press against the stitches and make them hurt more. Besides, the cap would be easier to spot at a distance. Not that Tommy would be at school. He must have been suspended, which would be ironic since he had actually told the truth for once. I reminded myself he would have plowed into Parvani instead if I hadn't intervened. It eased my conscience.

"Mrs. Hyde-Smith called while you were in the shower," Mom said. "Parvani isn't feeling well. So I'll be driving today." Exhaustion etched Mom's face. I think we both wanted to go back to bed. I certainly did, since the pain in the back of my head had kept me up most of the night.

English passed without incident. I took notes for Salem, and wondered how she was faring in Massachusetts.

It began to sprinkle after History. Not enough to cancel Capture the Flag, but enough to make me decide to sit out Gym in the nurse's office. I didn't care if the lights emitted a high pitched, mosquito-like buzz, or the cot mattress was about a half-inch thick and laid over a wood platform. My cheek hit the little airline-like pillow and I slipped into a deep, dreamless sleep.

The bell shrilled, jarring me awake. My head pounded as I walked to Spanish.

Señora Allende clucked over me. "Evie. *Espero que tu se sienta mejor pronto.*"

"*Gracias.* I hope I get better soon, too." I still faced two make up quizzes.

I had planned to study math during lunch, but instead I napped with my head down on a desk in Mr. Ross's room.

"Evie?"

I opened one eye. "Zhù, what are you doing here? Don't you have rehearsal?"

He gave me one of those lower-your-voice looks and glanced at Mr. Ross, who sat at his desk eating a turkey-and-cranberry sandwich.

"Mom is picking me up in five minutes. Parvani told me what happened in Gym the other day. You okay?"

I sat up. "Parvani is talking to you again?"

Zhù stared down at his feet. "Not exactly. She sent me a text message."

"Still. It's mondo progress." Hope sparked like fireworks. "See, I told you she likes you."

"So where is she?"

"Her mom said she wasn't feeling well this morning." I stifled a yawn. "You know what would cheer her up?"

"What?"

"Ask her to the Halloween dance."

Zhù slid his thumbs under the straps of his backpack. "Yeah. Right."

"I'm serious. Give her a call when you get home tonight."

"I'll think about it." He glanced at the door. "I better split."

"Okay. Later."

Despite being on the outs with Jordan and Parvani, my optimism rallied. Then the bell rang, a death toll reminding me it was time for Algebra and the make up quiz. Time to plummet into Loserville.

CHAPTER TWENTY-SEVEN

The math classroom stank of damp wool. Several kids wore knitted caps, the kind from Peru that hide your hair and have two braided ties that hang down to your chest. Maybe at high altitude the alpacas, or llamas, or whatever the caps were made of smelled okay in the rain. Not here.

My stomach grumbled from nerves and lack of food. I should have eaten my peanut butter and jelly sandwich, or at least a protein bar.

Before I could slink off to the back row, Mr. Bentley slammed a quiz down on a desk in the front. "Sit down and take this, O'Reilly, before class gets going."

A flush burned my cheeks. "But…"

"Hurry up."

I slid into the chair, despair settling like cement into every muscle and vein. When I leaned over to pull a pencil out of my backpack, the gash in the back of my head throbbed. I managed to write my name and the date in the right hand corner of the paper. I tried to recall the note Jordan had left explaining about graphs, but the information must have seeped out before Dr. Cameron stitched me up. It was gone. All gone.

I wanted to cry. I couldn't concentrate. I couldn't surreptitiously count on my fingers. Students walked past my desk, talking, distracting me. Chairs scraped. Books thudded open. Worse, the room quieted and I was sure all eyes were upon me.

I could already picture the scarlet F scrawled across the test. I had finished maybe half of the quiz when Mr. Bentley snapped his fingers in my face.

"Time's up, O'Reilly. Hand it over."

I hate math teachers.

When class ended, I blinked back tears and fled to Yearbook. Thirty-five of the first forty-one pages had already been set. Everyone huddled around me as I inserted the flash drive into the computer and brought up the photos Zhù had edited. Parvani's shot of the Goth, the prep, and the pixie elicited lots of smiles. Good thing, since we were light on fashion photos.

When I clicked on my pictures of Nazario and Pilar, Mia squealed. "Awesome!"

Miss Roberts leaned forward. "Evie, did you take these?"

"Yeah." Man, they were good. The loser slime from Algebra slid off me. I sat up straighter.

"Excellent," Miss Roberts said. "Layout artists, get to it. You've got some great photos to work with. Copy editors, get writing. Forty minutes 'til deadline."

The time flew by in a happy rush. Afterward, walking to Science, I wondered if Jordan would be there. *I should have asked Zhù if he'd seen him in HG.*

"There you are, Evie." Mr. Esenberg seemed pleased to see me. "Feeling better?"

"A little."

"Great." He thrust a quiz in my hand. "Take this to the teacher's lounge. I've arranged for a proctor to time you. You'll have twenty minutes."

"Okay." At least I'd have quiet and some privacy. I glanced at Jordan's empty chair. My worry meter pinged. If Jordan hadn't shown up by the time I returned, I'd bury my pride and call him. What if something awful had happened?

What if Parvani screwed up the spell?

Halfway between the faculty restrooms and the cafeteria, I spotted a puke-green door marked Teacher's Lounge. My heart beat a quick staccato. I was about to enter forbidden territory. Palms sweaty, I opened the door and crossed the threshold.

To my surprise, the place was empty. The room reeked of microwave sweet-and-sour chicken, reminding me I had skipped lunch. Two large windows let in plenty of light despite the overcast sky. An older model white refrigerator hummed next to a stainless steel counter. Dirty coffee mugs littered the sink. *I guess teachers can't afford take-out lattés.*

Three round tables took up most of the space. I wondered if teachers sat in cliques, with the cool teachers at one table, the nerdy, by-the-book teachers at another, and the loners huddled off to the side with their laptops. Speaking of teachers, where was my proctor?

The door flew open behind me. A sour, evil smell scythed the air and a bone-chilling draft whooshed in. The quiz paper slipped from my hand and skidded under a nearby chair.

"Better pick it up, Miss O'Reilly. The clock is ticking. You have twenty minutes."

Maybe it was my low blood sugar. Maybe it was six years of failure and humiliation in math. Maybe I was just having a wretched week and Miss Ravenwood had once tried to steal Dad from Mom. Whatever the reason, I rebelled.

I picked up my quiz and took a seat. A venomous entity rose within me and gave Miss Ravenwood a basilisk death stare. She blinked in surprise, then sat down at another table. I stared at her for a few more heartbeats. She returned my stare with her watery blue eyes and fiddled with the cuffs of her gray silk blouse. Her long, black skirt was so turn of the century — the nineteenth century. *She should hire Parvani to design some new clothes.*

A long breath escaped my lips. *Okay, Jordan.* I pictured his smile, and thought about how much I loved his joy and athletic grace when he rode his board. I visualized the binder paper he had left for me on the coffee table. In my mind, I opened it and read his notes. Keys began to unlock. The questions on the quiz made sense.

Hope flushed the concrete from my muscles and veins.

***

"Time." Miss Ravenwood rose from her chair, her back so straight I wondered if she had a broomstick for a spine. She thrust out her hand. Crumbs of dried wax had hardened beneath her fingernails.

Candle magic?

I handed over the quiz, praying Mom would forgive me for wrecking the family's good name if I had blown it. Forcing my chin up and my shoulders back, I headed for the door. My hand touched the silver handle when a bony claw clasped my shoulder.

"You didn't stop her."

Chills zigzagged like lightning bolts down my spine. "Stop who?"

"Miss Hyde-Smith. I warned her not to fool with matters she knows nothing about." Acid crept into Miss Ravenwood's voice.

I wrenched free and faced her. A wispy lock of frizzy black hair had fallen across her cheek.

"You'd better check on your friend. I believe he is most unwell." Miss Ravenwood's long skirt swished as she swept past me. The door shut behind her with an ominous click.

I blinked at the puke-green portal. *He.* Miss Ravenwood had said, "I believe *he* is most unwell."

Oh no. Jordan.

CHAPTER TWENTY-EIGHT

I ran across the wet field after class and threw myself into the front seat of the Volvo.

Mom lowered her romance novel. "Give me a heart attack, why don't you?"

I drew air into my lungs. "Sorry. Can we stop by Jordan's house on the way home?"

Mom crinkled her forehead. "Why? What's up?"

"He missed school, and I'm worried he's in trouble."

Mom switched on the ignition. "Why do you think he's in trouble?"

I wanted to say, "Because I think Parvani did a spell on him and something went wrong." Or, "Miss Ravenwood might have put a hex on him to spite us." Instead, I said, "Because he was supposed to come over on Sunday and he never showed. I think he's been absent all week."

She reached for her cell phone. "Maybe we should call him."

"Please, Mom." I yanked the scrunchie from my hair. "Can't we go to his house?"

Mom sighed. "Okay." She pulled out into traffic and did a U-turn at the next cross street. Jordan lived two blocks from Mr. Ross, in a tree-lined neighborhood not far from our old elementary school. When we reached his street, my heart revved like I'd been mainlining caffeine. Bright yellow leaves littered the lawn and the plywood skateboard ramp on the driveway. Mom parked next to the sidewalk, barely pulling to a stop before I jumped out.

"Be right back," I called over my shoulder.

The engine cut. I sprinted to the maroon-painted front door. In case Jordan was sick and trying to sleep, I knocked instead of ringing the bell. Rocking on my heels, I inhaled the spicy scent of rain-bathed cypress.

As I debated whether to knock again or leave, faint footsteps sounded within the house. The door swung open, and I came face to face with Jordan. The smell of day-old perspiration assaulted my nose. Not regular boy sweat. Fever sweat.

"Evie? What are you doing here?" He made a weak attempt to finger-comb his tangled hair, then lowered his arm as if he hadn't the strength to keep it aloft.

"Checking on you." My gaze worried across his glassy eyes and gaunt, ashen face, then dropped to his white tee and navy flannel pants. "Did I wake you?"

A faint hint of color bloomed on his cheeks. "Nah. Parvani woke me when she called around noon."

My brain stuttered. Parvani had called?

"I was worried when you didn't show up on Sunday."

"You didn't call me," he said.

"You stood me up. Shouldn't you have been the one to call?"

Jordan sighed like I had blown it. "I gotta go." He reached for the door and started to close it.

I blocked his way. "I'm sorry. But for all I knew, you had gone off to see Bucky What's-his-face again."

Jordan sagged against the doorjamb as if he were too weak to stand without support. "I had food poisoning."

"From the VFW breakfast?"

"Guess so."

"Wow. From pancakes and sausages? Is your grandfather okay?"

"He didn't get it. No one got it but me."

"Maybe it wasn't food poisoning." *Maybe it's your body fighting Parvani's spell.*

"Something sure hit me. The doctor said it isn't the flu."

It was Parvani. Or maybe Miss Ravenwood. No, Parvani. I felt like someone had piled the Guardian Stones upon my chest. "I'm sorry I jumped to the wrong conclusion. I should have called you."

"Thanks." Fatigue shadowed his lake blue eyes. "It isn't always about you, Evie."

I winced at the disappointment in his voice. Now *I* wanted to vomit. I swung around.

"Hey. What happened to your head?"

My fingers flew to my stitches. "An accident in Gym. Didn't Parvani tell you? I ended up in the hospital."

"Man, Evie. Parvani didn't say a word. She just called to check on me, then asked about the dance."

The Guardian Stones tumbled to my stomach, making room for the knife piercing my heart. "The dance?"

"Evie…"

"I'll email you my science notes." I dashed to the Volvo, fighting back tears.

"What happened?" Mom asked.

I fumbled with my seatbelt. "Food poisoning. He'll live." I stared straight ahead.

Mom hesitated, then switched on the ignition. We passed wine-colored plum trees and birches with their snowy trunks.

No willows. I was done with willows, and wands, and trolls, and Buddhas, and best friends.

And boys. I was definitely done with boys.

CHAPTER
TWENTY-NINE

Thursday morning, Mrs. Hyde-Smith called with some lame excuse to suspend carpooling. Fine by me. I had concluded Jordan was the major victim here, and I did not want to be in the same school with Parvani, much less share a car. Besides, the quiet drive gave me time to think about Dad and the looming anniversary of his death.

Mom seemed preoccupied. I got the feeling she didn't want to be home alone. Guess the extra trips to school were what Nana would call a blessing in disguise.

Friday dawned cool, clear, and sparkling after a night's rain. Wayward gulls called to each other overhead as I crossed the soggy field.

"Evie! Wait up."

My stomach flip-flopped at the sound of Jordan's voice. "Hey," I said when he fell into step beside me. "You're back."

The quick sprint had winded him. "Hey," he gasped.

His vampire-like pallor worried me. "Shouldn't you be home? You don't look too well."

"I wanted to be here. Where's Parvani?"

I wanted to slug him, but then I remembered it was the spell talking, not him. Besides, in his condition, even one of my swats might knock him flat.

"Haven't seen her." I tried to sound neutral, but snarkiness laced my voice. "We're not carpooling anymore."

"Wretched. Okay. See you in Gym." He squelched off.

Heat flamed from my throat to my strawberry hairline. I wondered if I could talk Mom into driving me to Well-Read Books. Karma be damned. I needed a counter spell.

By third period, the sun ruled the sky. Coach Willis blew his plastic whistle and yelled, "Mile time, people. Get running. Evie, Evan, hit the bleachers. No blood this time."

I felt like a rock in the middle of a river as my classmates streamed around me, headed for the outer edge of the field. Before I could gloat over Parvani having to run, I spotted her swing of long black hair. She jogged beside Jordan. My gloat soured into something ulcerous. Lacking options, I headed for the aluminum bleachers. Evan clumped ahead at a laborious limp, his right foot encased in a black walking cast. A twinge of guilt slowed my step.

Rainwater had pooled between the ridges of the aluminum, leaving just a three-foot dry patch under a redwood tree. Evan got there first. His face contorted as he shifted sideways and stretched his injured leg onto the bench.

Which left no room for me.

As I approached, Evan started to move his leg.

"No, no," I said, shocked by his unexpected gesture. I grabbed his leg to keep it from sliding off the bench. "Stay. I can stand."

"You have a concussion. You shouldn't stand all period."

"But you're in pain." Evan shrugged. His copper hair, clean for once, fell across his blue-gray eyes. "We'll compromise. I'll sit, and you put your leg across my lap."

His eyes lit up, igniting a moment of panic. Had I gone insane? Maybe my head injury was worse than I thought. I couldn't take back the words, so I lifted Evan's cast-encased foot and sat down. "This thing weighs a ton," I said after he lowered the cast onto my lap.

"Tell me about it."

"I'm sorry…" We spoke at the same time and stared at each other in surprise.

"I didn't mean to break your foot."

"I swear I had nothing to do with Tommy mowing you down."

I tried to remember if I had ever seen Evan without Tommy. The class thundered past. A couple of guys hooted. Someone yelled, "Way to go, MacDonald."

Then the stragglers jogged past. Shock played across Parvani's face. Jordan slowed to a near stop and stared. My heart freefell when I registered his confused expression.

"You call yourself a running back, Kent? Even the girls are passing you," Evan chided.

Jordan flashed me a hurt look. My heart tore. I glared at Parvani. She lowered her chin and averted her gaze, but not before I spied the remorse in her eyes. She knew she had screwed up big time, but didn't know how to fix things.

Kind of how I'd felt when Dad died.

I glanced back at Jordan. His lake-blue eyes bored into me. I gulped a couple of times, my thoughts skittering. Someone bumped Jordan from behind. He stumbled forward, cast me a final, forlorn look, and then jogged on, leaving me alone with Evan, Smash Head.

CHAPTER THIRTY

The next eight days passed in a miserable blur.

"You have to do something." Zhù shouldered past me like a chocolate-seeking missile and headed right for the kitchen.

"And *buenas tardes* to you."

"Buenas tardes. Got a bowl?"

"What size?"

Zhù dumped his backpack on a chair and started to unzip it. "Cereal size will work."

I dragged a chipped bowl out of the cabinet and placed it on the table.

"Gracias." Zhù pulled out a baggie and poured a bunch of edamame into the bowl.

I stared at the little green spheres. "You don't like brownies anymore?"

Zhù tossed a bunch of soybeans into his mouth. "Love them. But I'm starving. Thought I'd start with these. Besides, soybeans help me think."

I brought over a plate of brownies and two glasses of water.

"Parvani won't talk to me," Zhù said.

"She's not speaking to me, either."

"She's been avoiding me ever since she saw me at your house. I still don't know what she meant by her comment."

"What comment?"

"She said, 'I expected more from you.'"

Guys. So clueless. I pulled out a chair and sat. "Parvani probably thought you'd always be there for her. You know, her loyal sidekick. Maybe she didn't realize how much you meant to her until she saw us together and she thought she'd lost you."

"That's crazy."

"No it's not."

Zhù sat down and popped five more beans into his mouth. After he swallowed, he said, "But she acted all crazy about Jordan. She even asked him to the dance."

The stones piled up on my heart again. "Because she was mad at us." *And insane.* "I told you to tell her the truth about your dancing."

"You know why I can't."

Risking a beating by the Smash Heads was a problem. Then again, so was directing a love spell at someone against his will. "Parvani needs your help," he continued. "Have you seen her? She looks worse than Jordan. Yesterday, she wore a belt that clashed with her shoes."

"Are you sure you're not gay?"

Zhù threw a bean at my forehead.

I plucked a couple of beans from the bowl and contemplated starting a food fight, but this was too serious. "I can't help her."

"Why not? She's your friend. Jordan is your friend. You have to do something. The dance is in six days."

Frost tinged my voice. "I'm well aware of how many days are left until Halloween."

Zhù paused mid-chew. I could see him flipping through his mental file marked *Evie*. He swallowed hard. "Your dad. I'm an idiot. How is your mom holding up?"

"She's on the phone all the time with Dad's agent." Anguish, raw as an untreated sore, welled within me. "Several of Dad's photos will be featured in a new anthology about the war."

"Hey, great."

I nodded, unable to speak.

Zhù fished his Spanish book out of his backpack and opened it.

"Hallie volunteered to photograph the dance," I said, changing the subject.

"Good. Then neither of us will have to go. Maybe I'll take Ming trick-or-treating."

"Cool. Dress as a ballet dancer and stop by Parvani's house first."

Zhù threw a couple more soybeans at me. This time I retaliated and bounced one off his glasses. It fell on the floor and Baby snapped it up.

After Zhù left, I sat on the floor and plowed my fingers through Baby's hair. "The sky will be dark tonight," I whispered. "It's the new moon. A ripe time for casting a counter-spell."

CHAPTER THIRTY-ONE

I figured it would take a pretty heavy-duty spell to counter the one Parvani had cast. I didn't want to wing it and risk possible karmic repercussions, or accidentally summon a demon or something.

The library was closed. None of the bookstores were within walking distance, and Mom was too busy working on her next batch of cards to drive me. I thought of searching online for info on spell busting, but Mom kept working at the kitchen table. Probably she didn't want to be alone, especially not in the studio. Not this week.

I needed to call an expert, which pretty much meant Miss Ravenwood, or Nana. I snuck off to my room and dialed Nana's number. She answered on the third ring. "Hi Nana. It's Evie."

"Hello, Precious. What a pleasant surprise. How are you?"

"Not so great, Nana. I need your help." I decided to just dive in. "Do you know how to counter a wrongful love spell?"

The line went silent.

"Nana, you there?"

"Yes, sorry. Just trying to recover."

"Mom told me you dabbled in the Craft. Can you help me?"

"How like Olivia. 'Dabbled.'" Nana snorted. "Sounds so frivolous. Who cast the spell?"

"A friend of mine."

"Then your friend has to be the one to undo it. Did this friend bind someone against their will?"

I thought of Jordan. "Yes."

"Terrible karma, kiddo."

"I know. I tried to warn her."

"She must be a new soul. Too bad about the boy, though."

"There has to be something I can do."

"Hmm. All I can think of is severing the spell link."

"Spell link?"

"It's a thin magical cord, like a vapor trail, left by the spell. It connects your friend to the boy. Severing it with a black-handled knife might set both of them free. But that's pretty advanced magic, being able to see a spell link."

"I haven't noticed it so far. Besides, I'll get expelled if I run around school with a knife, black-handled or otherwise."

"I'm sorry, Precious. I don't know what else to tell you."

"Thanks anyway, Nana. If you think of anything else, call me, okay?"

"Promise. Love you."

"Love you, too." I hung up and put on Dad's cap. I could use some luck, or a miracle.

The rest of the weekend dragged. My Worry Meter hovered between Meltdown and Calm-Down-Or-You'll-Die. I wondered what effect Parvani's casting had had on *Teen Wytche?* Had the book shrunk? Grown horns? Did it pulse like a broken heart?

At school, I watched Jordan and Parvani, searching for the spell link. If it was there, I sure couldn't see it. As the days passed, the spell's repercussions became more evident. Jordan and I resorted to doing our lab work during lunch, since the spell seemed to prevent him from coming to my house. First, he'd injured his leg during football play-offs, so he couldn't skateboard over. Then his mom had had a series of committee meetings for a fall fundraiser, so he'd had to stay home and watch his grandfather. So we worked in Mr. Ross's room while Parvani sat nearby, pretending to study Honors Geometry.

No sign of the spell link.

Dejected, I took down my Shay Stewart shrine and burned the photos in fireplace. Baby snored on the rag rug while I hung up the laundry piled on my floor. Anything that had lain there for more than two weeks I tossed in the washer. Parvani would have been pleased.

Halloween and the anniversary of Dad's death loomed. I missed having a best friend to talk to. If only Parvani would undo the spell — I missed her and Jordan. Nothing seemed right. Salem hadn't called or come home, either.

I cleared off my desk and dusted it. Then I dug through boxes of old photos until I found the shot of Jordan and me at Disneyland with Excalibur. I put it in a silver frame next to a picture of Mom and Dad.

Nana called. Mom lied and told her we were fine. "Any luck?" Nana asked when I got on the phone.

"None"

"Sorry, kiddo."

"Me too, Nana."

On Halloween Eve, the doorbell rang. My heart leapt. *Jordan? Parvani? Salem?* I raced behind Baby, but Mom got to the door first.

"Hi, I'm Lilith, Sarah Miller's cousin." She appeared about nineteen, and sported a buzz-cut the left side of her head. The hair on her right side grazed her jaw. "I'm in cosmetology school," she explained. "Sarah said Evie wanted back her natural hair color. It won't cost you anything. I need the practice hours to graduate."

Mom gaped.

Lilith held out a bulging tote bag. "I brought all my stuff. Are you free? I should have called, but I lost your phone number. All I could remember was the address."

"Well, um." Mom raised her eyebrows at me.

I clasped Mom's hand and held it to my heart. For added measure, I blinked several times and did my best wounded-puppy impression. "Please? If she does it right, I'll look like my old self again." *I'll look more like Dad.*

Doubt and hope warred in Mom's eyes. Would Lilith fry my hair? Turn it magenta? My strawberry roots were two inches long — things couldn't get much worse. I took off Dad's cap and pointed to my outgrowth. "Can you get me back to this color?"

Lilith poked her tongue against the inside of her cheek. I got a brief glance at her silver tongue stud. "Sure thing. The results will be pure magic."

Mom sighed. "Okay. Come in."

***

When I woke the next morning, my mind was on Jordan and *Teen Wytche.* So when I entered the bathroom and confronted my reflection in the mirror, my heart jolted. Dad's blue eyes stared back at me, framed by his strawberry blonde hair. *No wonder Mom teared up last night when Lilith was finished.* I blew out a long breath. This was going to take some getting used to, especially today.

Halloween.

"The art crowd and Goths dress up and hold sort of an anti-dance in the quad at lunch," I told Mom over breakfast. "I have to cover it for Yearbook."

"You're going to take pictures?"

"If I don't freak again. Wish me luck."

She kissed my forehead like I was a little kid or something. Her lips were soft and reassuring, and her mom smell engulfed me. "Good luck, sweetie. I know you'll do fine."

"How about you?" I asked. "Because Hallie can cover the ghouls if…"

"No need for you to worry. Baby will keep me company. Now get dressed. We're falling behind schedule."

I got moving. I figured it was Halloween, the best possible time to detect a spell trail.

At Jefferson, unlike middle school, students didn't have to wait until last period to don their costumes. We were, however, forbidden to wear fake or actual weapons. So, of course, no black-handled knives allowed. Middle school had the same rule. It had always posed a problem for the Smash Heads.

In English, a quiet and unassuming girl who sat to my right showed up in a black-and-red corseted Goth fairy costume. I had never seen her in anything other than a sweatshirt and jeans. Who knew she had cleavage? I kept wondering if she was freezing in her miniskirt and black spider web tights. Even Mrs. Knapp seemed to find her distracting, and kept losing her train of thought mid-sentence. Having everyone hyped up on purloined candy and anticipation didn't help.

In Gym, failure to wear a Wildcats gym shirt, even on Halloween, could result in a grade drop. So there we stood, thirty-seven freshmen packed into the multipurpose room. A guy smeared with fake blood, wearing vampire teeth, and a green mesh gym shirt hurled a dodge ball at me.

Psycho.

Jordan and Parvani entered my peripheral vision. It may have been my imagination but, when I squinted and blocked the glare of the gym lights, I thought I saw a pale blue cord connecting Parvani's heart to Jordan's back. *The spell link!* Was it some sort of Halloween trick? Had the concoction Lilith had smeared on my hair given me super powers?

It didn't matter. I needed to sever the link.

Jordan's athletic grace and his warm, inclusive smile were gone. His lake-blue eyes had dulled to a stormy gray. He seemed lost, as if he couldn't remember how to play the game — or any game.

Parvani's perfect posture had abandoned her. Shoulders hunched, she shrank. She had twisted her thick black hair into a haphazard bun held together by two yellow pencils. In place of her designer frames, she wore her rimless glasses from seventh grade. Karma had kicked her in the teeth. Watching her and Jordan, my stomach burned. There had to be a way to cut the spell link without using a lethal weapon.

The answer didn't appear to me, not even in Spanish where I tend to be brilliant. When the lunch bell sounded, I raced to Yearbook to retrieve a camera from Miss Roberts. By the time I walked back down the ramp, *Thriller* blared from speakers in the quad. I followed the driving beat, encountering the pixie from Parvani's French class.

"Amazing Corpse Bride costume!" I said, snapping her picture.

She made her eyes huge. "Tim Burton rules."

In each picture I took, at least one of the obnoxious orange posters for the Halloween dance appeared in the background. I fought the urge to tear them down. *In the future, I think the social committee should channel their revolting energy and enthusiasm toward a better cause. I vote for world peace.*

Distracted, I didn't notice the sudden drop in temperature or the stench of evil until I almost crashed into Miss Ravenwood. She'd painted her face green and wore a tall witch's hat. For a heart-stopping minute, her gaze roved over my newly restored hair color. Her stern expression crumpled.

"You look like Deaman."

"I know."

Miss Ravenwood swallowed. Her lips curled inward, almost disappearing. Regret and grief welled in her eyes. I realized then what my father must have meant to her. My heart constricted.

The brimstone smell faded. "Miss Hyde-Smith and Mr. Kent are flunking Honors Geometry," Miss Ravenwood said in a shaky voice.

"They are?" I imagined she'd broken some major privacy rule by telling me.

She leaned closer, giving me a good view of the fake wart on her nose. "They need your help."

"I'm in remedial math."

"A different kind of help, Miss O'Reilly." Her gaze pierced me like a pin through a butterfly. The flecks in her watery blue eyes darkened. In that moment, I knew. Miss Ravenwood had once cast a binding love spell and had suffered similar results. I had the uneasy feeling my father had been the recipient.

I wondered if Mom knew.

"Karma," Miss Ravenwood said, her brow arching. She swept off in a rustle of long skirts.

"Yours, or theirs?" I called after her.

She angled her head, displaying a razor-edged profile. "Yes."

I wanted to stomp my feet in frustration. At the last minute, I whipped the camera to my eye and shot Miss Ravenwood's striped stockings and ruby heels before she disappeared.

I followed the pounding Michael Jackson beat to the pale standing stones and sticky benches ringing the quad. A black-winged fairy of the night danced with a freshman steampunk aviator. A blonde senior dressed in a body-hugging designer dress and four-hundred-dollar stilettos I had seen in a department store window wore a Trophy Wife sign beneath her diamond necklace. She danced with Nazario, dressed as himself. Knowing Mia would be hurt, I didn't take their picture. Instead, I shot an overenthusiastic Raggedy Ann as she jumped on the back of a boy with vampire fangs, dressed as a surgeon.

My heart plummeted like a falling star when Jordan lurched by, dressed as a zombie. Parvani walked a few paces behind him, bedecked in a feather headdress. From the hip up, she was encased in a gilded cage. It was her most spectacular design yet. Awed, I ran ahead to photograph her. I had to twist past a Goth eating a burrito in order to angle the photo so the spell vapor wouldn't be visible. I should have taken Jordan's picture as well, but I couldn't. I just couldn't.

Thriller ended with zombie groans, a falsetto scream, and an evil laugh. After a pause, Beethoven's Fifth blared from the speakers. *Not your typical dance music...* I lowered my camera. After some confused swearing from the Goths, the focus shifted to a lithe form on the side of the quad. Parvani had rotated around to catch the spectacle. She gasped at the same time I did.

Zhù had skipped his Nutcracker rehearsal. His cut-at-the-midriff muscle tee revealed his sculpted biceps, and abs rivaling those of the cover models on Mom's romance novels. The hem of his charcoal sweatpants ended at the ankle, revealing black ballet slippers.

The Smash Heads, Tommy in the lead, shouldered their way into the crowd. My stomach clenched. I had wanted Zhù to tell Parvani about his dancing, not to sign his own death warrant.

Tommy, whose vague attempt at costuming consisted only of zipper scars across his cheeks and hands, grabbed a freshman's butterfly wings and flapped them as she shrieked. Evan ignored him and scanned the crowd. His glance flicked from me to Zhù. I willed Evan to look back at me. He did, and we held each other's gazes.

Please, I silently pleaded.

The music stopped, plunging the quad into sudden silence. Evan had dressed like Shay Stewart's famous pirate role. He looked good. I held my breath and waited.

"Yo ho, yo ho," Evan sang. Some of the crowd joined in, proving there must have been a lot of the drama club and chorus kids among the sullen Goths.

Tommy's eyes lit like a hyena spotting a zebra with a limp.

Evan tried to dance a little pirate jig which, given his cast, was either Herculean or foolhardy. I didn't care. It took everyone's attention off Zhù.

Except Parvani's. She tried to make her way to Zhù. I know she tried. But the spell kept her tethered to Jordan, and he had slumped onto a bench.

Looking dejected, Zhù slipped away. As I watched him go, I wondered how much worse things would have to get before Parvani would reverse the spell.

CHAPTER THIRTY-TWO

Mom gunned the Volvo up our street. "So, just you and me tonight?"

I hugged her arm, grateful she'd remained the same, no matter how much havoc the love spell caused with everyone else. "You, me, Baby, and who knows how many superheroes, firemen and princesses. Can we order pizza?"

"Again? Sure. Let's eat early. Just like the old days." Her smile faded and I knew she was thinking about Dad. He hovered between us, a ghost, stirring old memories and ripping open fresh guilt. Mom and I had just sat down to a thick crust, double cheese pizza when the doorbell rang. "It's too early for trick-or-treaters," we said at the same time.

Mom wiped her mouth with a napkin. "I'll get it." She grabbed the bowl of candy and headed with Baby toward the entry.

I didn't hear the usual Halloween yells, just quiet conversation and footsteps heading my way. A familiar Goth appeared, *sans* makeup and dressed in jeans and a subdued knit top.

"You're back!" I hugged Sarah, which surprised me as much as it did her.

"Sit," Mom commanded.

Sarah pulled out a chair. Baby sat on the floor.

"Did they feed you on the plane?"

Sarah snorted. "No, though we were free to purchase boxed gag-me lunches."

Mom reached for the cupboard. "I'll grab another plate."

"I like your hair," Sarah said.

"Lilith did it. And look at yours. It's so long."

"I should call Lilith. Maybe change my image. Everyone looks so Goth these days."

"It's called Halloween," I informed her.

Sarah swatted me with Mom's greasy napkin.

"Can you stay for awhile?" I asked.

"Okay with you, Mrs. O'Reilly?" Sarah asked.

"Of course. Spend the night if you'd like. We could use the company."

I squeezed Mom's hand. I knew she had expected to have a quiet, sad Halloween, just the two of us.

Sarah and I were too excited to polish off the pizza, so Mom said, "I'll listen for trick-or-treaters if you two want to go to Evie's room and catch up."

"Are you sure?"

Mom waved her hand. "Go. I'll finish my novel. I'm at the good part."

We took off while she boxed up the pizza and put it in the refrigerator. As soon as the bedroom door closed behind us, Sarah dove onto the nearest twin bed. "Okay, O'Reilly. Spill everything."

I plopped into the beanbag chair and regurgitated all the depressing details.

"You saw the spell link?" Sarah said when I finished.

I nodded. "But I couldn't do anything about it. Which means it's still up to Parvani to fix this, which she won't, since she's at the dance with Jordan."

"I don't get it. It sounds like neither of them is happy. Why doesn't she do something?"

"She might be too rattled to try anything else," I said. "Especially if *Teen Wytche* doesn't list a counter spell."

The doorbell rang. Baby barked in the kitchen.

"I better get Baby and lock her up in here with us. Mom will have her hands full with the candy."

"Good idea. May I use your restroom?"

"Go for it."

I rounded the corner near the entry and saw Mom kneeling before the open door. The tricksters must be little kids. They always came out first.

Baby stood beside Mom, tail wagging, poking her nose into the candy bowl.

"Bye!" Mom stood and waved.

I stepped on the cracked tile, wincing as it crunched beneath my feet. Mom pivoted, one hand on the door, the other holding the orange candy bowl. "Evie. Someone is here to see you."

She stepped back and headed for the kitchen.

Curious, I peeked around the door. "Parvani?"

She adjusted her glasses. "May I come in?"

"Sure. Where is your costume? I thought you were going to the dance." *With Jordan.*

"I decided not to go. Is Salem back yet?"

"Yeah. She stopped by a little while ago and stayed for dinner. Why?"

"I need your help — both of you."

My hopes skyrocketed. I angled my head toward my room. "Come on." I let her lead, so I could sneak a quick look outside before I closed the door. Darn. No Jordan. He couldn't be too far away, not with the spell link.

We met Sarah in the hall as she came out of the bathroom. "Parvani. You look like something Einstein threw up."

"Gee, thanks, Sarah."

I gave her a meaningful look. "Parvani wants our help with something."

Sarah raised a studded brow. We filed back into my room and closed the door. Parvani knelt on the rag rug and slid her backpack off her shoulder.

"What's up?" I asked.

"This." Parvani pulled out *Teen Wytche*. It had shrunken and shriveled. The silver foliage on the cover now resembled dry, dead leaves. The plum leather had cracked, and the edges weren't leather at all.

"It's reverting back," I said.

"Oh no!" Sarah took the tome from Parvani and caressed the cover. She bit her lip as she opened it, then drew in a sharp breath when she saw the pages. Little remained of the handwritten spidery scrawl on vellum. Most of the pages had begun to change back to machine-printed text on paper. "Dear Goddess."

"It coughed filthy cobwebs all over my twelve-hundred dollar handbag, and tried to set fire to my favorite flats." Parvani sobbed. "I'm so sorry, Evie. I saw how much Jordan liked you, and then I thought you'd stolen Zhù… I don't know. I wrecked everything. Now Jordan's miserable, and I'm miserable, and you're not speaking to me, and I've been too ashamed to talk to Zhù. My grades are suffering and Dad's upset because I've blown the BMCR…"

"What's a BMCR?" Sarah asked. She waved her hand. "Never mind. I don't care."

"Building my college résumé," I explained anyway.

Parvani sniffed. "I don't know how to undo this mess."

"What if Parvani revokes the spell," I asked Sarah, "then casts a new one, where she asks for the qualities she wants in her true love? Will that fix things?"

Sarah hugged *Teen Wytche* to her chest. "It might, if we word it right."

Parvani sniffed. "Do you think so?"

I handed her a tissue. "Breathe. You need to be calm for spell casting, remember?"

Parvani nodded and blew her nose. "I brought all the things I used to cast the original spell." She opened her backpack and pulled out the knife, the Buddha statue, and the rest. "I already used up the pink candle."

"You used pink instead of red? Thank the Goddess," Sarah said.

"Why, what's the difference?" I asked.

"Um, level of intensity."

A blush spread across Parvani's cheeks, which more than ever resembled a rich, French roast coffee, no cream or sugar.

"Evie, do you have any white candles?" Sarah asked. "They can stand in for pink."

"We have a bag of white tea lights. I'll go get them."

When I returned, I left Baby out in the hall. Inside my room, the overhead light had been turned off. The reading lamp on my desk shed a small pool of light, plunging most of the room into darkness. The circle was set. I noticed a slightly crinkled photo of Jordan in the center. It showed him in profile, midair on his skateboard, his hair windblown. He seemed oblivious to the camera, and I wondered if Parvani had taken the shot with her cell phone.

Sarah scribbled something on a piece of binder paper. When she saw me, she paused and handed each of us a scrap of paper.

"Write down the qualities you'd most like in a boyfriend," she commanded. The three of us hunched over my desk to catch the scant illumination.

"First we undo the original spell." Sarah placed a tea light on top of each Guardian Stone, and lit them as she called in the guardians of the four directions to aid and protect us. As the ritual continued, my breath slowed. The doorbell, the dog's barks, and shouts of trick-or-treat faded.

"I release thee, Jordan Campbell Kent," Parvani said aloud three times as she read from Sarah's notes. "And I ask forgiveness from your higher self for binding you against your will. I ask to clear on all planes any negative karma this may have caused."

"So mote it be." Sarah rang a little silver bell she had found in my hutch.

Just to be sure, I picked up the black-handled knife and sliced the air where the spell link had been. Blue light crackled up the blade, reached the hilt, and gave me a major case of pins and needles. "So mote it be." I placed the knife on the floor. We stood in silence for a moment.

"Now let's do the spell the right way, so you can find your true love," I said.

"Not just me," Parvani protested. "All of us."

We lifted our binder paper to the candlelight, and one by one we read our lists and said the magic words. *Kind, smart,* and *cute* appeared on all three lists. I included *compassionate.* Parvani listed *tenacious, loyal,* and *likes ballet.* Salem had written *creative* and *a major wit.*

I heard a small poof, then breathed in a spicy caravan and campfires aroma. A tingle tiptoed across my shoulders then danced down my arms. Somewhere outside the sacred circle, tiny pewter bells chimed.

CHAPTER THIRTY-THREE

After the ritual we sat on the floor within the circle, our faces illuminated by the candlelight. My thoughts drifted to Mom, then Dad.

"Didn't you say Samhain is a good time to honor the dead?" I asked Sarah.

"It is. Would you like to do something for your father?"

"We should!" Parvani gushed. "But first, Sarah, I want to give you something." She lifted *Teen Wytche* off the makeshift altar and handed it to her.

Sarah gaped as though she'd just been handed a rare treasure, and pressed her hand to the grimoire's tattered cover. The book pulsed as though resuscitated. "Are you sure?"

"Yes!" Parvani and I said in unison.

"Wow. Thanks."

"I'll go get Mom. She should be part of our ritual for Dad."

Sarah nodded. "I'll hold the sacred space. And, you know, I think from now on I want to be called Salem. It feels right, all of a sudden."

"It suits you," Parvani said.

I stepped out into the hall, almost tripping over Baby, who had fallen asleep outside my door. I was unsure of how much time had passed. It must have gotten late enough to turn out the porch light and snag Mom.

The doorbell rang, blowing my theory. Baby's paw quivered, but she remained in doggie dreamland. I started down the hall with Parvani in my wake.

"I'll get it," she said. "Find your mom."

We reached the entry together, and Parvani opened the front door. "Zhù!" Parvani threw her arms around him.

Zhù's jaw dropped an inch. He stood riveted in the porch light, Mom's jack-o-lantern flickering at his feet. Then he closed his eyes and hugged Parvani.

I left them alone and went to check on Mom.

"Hey." I came up behind her in the kitchen as she reached for the candy bowl and slid my arms around her waist. "Zhù's at the door. I think he and Parvani have made up."

Mom patted my hand. "I'm so glad."

"Any pizza left?" a familiar male voice asked.

I swung toward the sound, my heart leapfrogging. "Jordan!"

His eyes had a disoriented, post-spell glaze. He held out his arms. "Evie." He managed to convey love, need, apology, relief, and joy all in the way he said my name.

I melted into his arms. The chill night air clung to him, so I tightened the embrace, willing my warmth to seep into him. He sighed against me and pressed his forehead to mine. His lips were so close…

"Ahem."

Mom! I had forgotten about her. Jordan and I eased apart.

He pulled out a chair and sank into it. "I'm starving. I can't remember the last time I ate." He plucked at his zombie costume, dazed. I leaned down and kissed him on the cheek. Jordan pressed his fingers to the spot.

I pulled the leftover pizza out of the fridge and handed it to him. "Don't go anywhere," I said. "I'll be right back."

I sprinted past Zhù and Parvani making out in the entry and dashed down the hall. Stepping over Baby, I entered my candlelit bedroom. "Jordan's here," I told Salem. "Hand me the knife."

Although she probably broke some "holding the sacred circle" rule, Salem passed me the black-handled knife.

"Thanks."

I returned to the brightly lit kitchen. Mom had joined Jordan at the table. Squinting, I saw a few ragged spell vapors still attached to Jordan's back, level with his heart. "Lean forward," I instructed, hiding the knife from view. "You have something on your costume."

Jordan bowed over the table.

Mom stood when she saw the knife, her eyes wide with confusion and alarm. "Evie…"

Blue light crackled up the blade as I sliced the air close to Jordan's back. The remnants of the spell link burst like popped bubbles. Jordan rolled his shoulders. "Wow. My skin just went all weird. What did you do?"

"Nothing." I shot Mom a quick glance before stashing the knife into the nearest drawer. Her shoulders relaxed a bit and she sat back down, but I could tell she'd have a few questions for me later. "Salem says it's a tradition on Samhain to honor those who have died. Would you two like to join me in a ritual for Dad?"

Mom's eyes misted. "What a great idea."

"Count me in," Jordan said.

"Great. Mom, could you grab a picture of Dad for the circle, and pull out the last photos he took in Afghanistan?"

"The ones you've refused to look at?"

"Yes." I inhaled a long breath, and released it. "I want to see them. They must have been important. Otherwise, Dad never would have risked his life to take them. Let's put them in the circle next to his lucky cap and a bar of his peppermint soap, if you still have one." I had a feeling *Teen Wytche* would like Dad's special smell.

"I'll go find them." Mom took off.

Jordan brushed his fingertips across the back of my hand, sending tingles sprinting up my arm. "Good call, Lois." He pulled me onto his lap.

I slid my arms around his neck and breathed in his familiar outdoorsy scent. "I'm glad you approve."

His eyes lit with the twinkle I had missed so much. His lips parted. "Oh, I approve." He closed his eyes and we both leaned in close for a tentative kiss.

I think my toes curled. I know my stomach fluttered. The scent of summer roses perfumed the room, and I'm pretty sure I heard the far-off tinkle of tiny pewter bells.

The End.

Turn the page to read an excerpt from

SPELL STRUCK

**The second book in the TEEN WYTCHE SAGA
by Ariella Moon**

Star Tribe Publishing

EXCERPT FROM SPELL STRUCK

My whole life since fifth grade has been a lie. That was when I razor-cut my blond hair and dyed it Ebony Nightfall and Passionately Purple. I got a silver eyebrow stud, which hurt like blazes, then became infected and hurt even worse. I scoured thrift shops for vintage black clothing and adopted a Mess-With-Me-At-Your-Own-Peril attitude. Teachers no longer recognized me as Amy Miller's little sister. I became the Anti-Amy. No resemblance, no expectations. And unfortunately, no friends.

Magic always exacts a price.

But now, barely three months into my freshman year at Jefferson High, I'd found a friend—Evie O'Reilly. She'd seen through my disguise and discovered the true reason behind it: I have difficulty reading and spelling.

Compared to Amy, I'm a huge failure. But earlier this Halloween night, I had succeeded at something big. I'd overturned a wrongful love spell. As a consequence, I totally saved a life, probably two. And I helped Evie in the process. I tightened my grip on the gift she had given me, an ever-morphing ancient spell book. My brain buzzed with the thought, *Tonight will definitely go in my Karmic Win column.*

Evie sat beside me in the back seat as her mom drove the few dark blocks separating our houses. Most porch lights had been extinguished to discourage late-night trick-or-treaters. My parents had remembered to leave ours on, and it shined like a beacon as the Volvo swung into my driveway and halted with a slight lurch.

"Bye, Salem," Evie said.

"Bye. Thanks for the ride, Mrs. O'Reilly." Giddy with success and magic, I hopped out, closed the car door, then waved to Evie before sprinting to the entranceway. The lantern-shaped light fixture cast an amber glow over the empty candy bowl perched on the footstool. As I unlocked the door, I wondered if the trick-or-treaters had heeded the Please Take One sign, or if marauding teens had stolen all the chocolates.

Feeling like a thief, I snuck inside. Einstein, Amy's cockapoo, guarded the marble entry. The dog ignored me and stood on his hind legs to sniff the recyclable bag looped over my wrist. One whiff of the noxious brimstone emanating from the half-destroyed spell book was enough to catapult him, nails clicking, down the hall. He raced past the half-bath on the right, my room on the left, then Amy's. He took the corner at a skid, almost crashed into the glass case displaying Amy's trophies, recovered, and then disappeared from view.

"Sarah?" It sounded as if Mom had cracked open my parents' bedroom door at the unseen end of the L-shaped hall.

My post-magic buzz vanished. I shielded the bag behind my back and froze. "Yeah, Mom," I called out. "I'm back from Evie's."

"Good night, Toothpick." Dad sounded exhausted. I pictured him standing behind Mom, dressed in his white tee shirt and gray flannel pajama bottoms. He was probably scratching the stubble along his jaw.

"Good night." I waited, muscles tensed. When neither of them emerged around the corner, my arm dropped to my side. The grimoire pressed against my thigh like an anxious toddler at a new preschool. My gaze migrated to my sister's bedroom door. Part of me wanted to sit on Amy's bed and hug her favorite stuffed animal, Flipper. *Would Amy get better? Should we have brought her home?* I thought about the suicide prevention pamphlet stuffed in my backpack. *Surely the Massachusetts Institute of Technology would permit a leave of absence for a student who had overdosed.*

She's going to get better. She has to.

In the hall, I hurried past the framed eight-by-ten photos of Amy. Thirteen years of formal school portraits, splashy action shots of Amy scoring for the water polo team, and Amy giving her valedictorian speech last June. In each, her shiny blond hair haloed her sun-kissed face. Her eyes gleamed with intelligence; her smile was wide and welcoming. She radiated athletic wholesomeness.

Interspersed among the photos of the Golden One were a few smaller photos of me. Well, photos of my pre-Goth self, taken when I'd looked like a mini-Amy but with an unsure smile, worried eyes, and fragility instead of athletic prowess. There were no pictures of me after the fifth grade. Zero. *Nada.* I had ceased to exist when I'd gone Goth.

I was shocked my parents had waited up for me tonight. *Maybe I'm the Golden One now.* The thought unsettled me. It wasn't like when I had been four and Amy eight, and we had played on the seesaw. Amy shouldn't have to teeter down for me to rise up. What kind of a victory would that be?

The hundred-watt light from my desk lamp spilled like a beacon into the hall. I gravitated toward it, tiptoeing to soften the thud of my faux combat boots against the parquet floor. Einstein doubled back and took up sentry in front of Amy's room.

"Behave," I whispered, entering my bedroom. As I locked the door behind me, the wounded spell book coughed up another cloud of brimstone. The stink bomb fanned out like cigarette smoke and coated my pearl-gray walls. *Great. Just great.* I tossed my keys onto the bed and watched them sink into the pale aqua comforter. I waited for the peacefulness of my un-Goth, Zen-like room to seep into my bones. As the new owner of a shape-shifting spell book, I needed as much tranquility as I could muster.

Biting my lip, I withdrew the volatile grimoire from the bag and carried it to the curved Japanese bench that served as my meditation altar. As I placed it next to my Kuan Yin statue, a fresh wave of anger rippled through me. *What had Parvani been thinking?* Evie had warned her not to direct a love spell at Jordan Kent. She had warned her to never direct a love spell at anyone. *Hello? It's called karma, you moron.*

Eventually, Parvani had caved. Earlier tonight we'd rescued Jordan, Evie's secret crush and the victim of Parvani's enchantment. But we'd been too late to save the spell book. When Evie had first bought the grimoire at a used bookstore, it had appeared to be an ordinary paperback titled *Teen Wytche*. Once she'd brought it home, the book had grown to the size of a photo album and all vestiges of the paperback had disappeared.

I had thought of Merlin, Morgan le Fay, and swords and sorcery when I'd first seen the plum leather cover with its embossed silver leaves and vines. Goosebumps erupted on my arms as I remembered the grimoire's vellum pages covered in spidery handwriting.

"What happened to you?" I whispered so my parents wouldn't hear. "Did your original owner cast a fail-safe spell on you in case you fell into the wrong hands?" I grimaced, imagining Parvani's desperate wrongful love spell launching a magical self-destruct code. The grimoire had shrunk. The edges of the leather cover had singed, then reverted to paper. Most of the shiny silver leaf had faded away. Nearly all of the handwritten vellum pages had disappeared, replaced by printed text on modern paper.

I sank to my knees and placed my hand on the tattered spell book. A fragment of the cover was still embossed leather. *Thump-thump. Thump-thump.* It beat like a failing heart against my hand.

My palm chakras pulsed. A weird push-pull charge thrust my hand off the grimoire, tethering it inches above the spell book. *Am I shoving healing in, or dragging dark energies out?* The magical tug-of-war whirled my stomach. Without warning, the cover swelled like a giant blister and emitted a jagged bolt of magical vomit.

"Flipping frogs!" I jerked my hand away and flicked the smoke-colored mojo to the floor, but I couldn't stop the odd compulsion rippling through me. Propelled to my desk, I scavenged through the top drawer until I found a silver permanent marker. With quick, exact strokes, I drew the silver leaf design on my left wrist. Just three leaves, but they matched the ones on the grimoire. The sting from the discharged magic subsided.

I expelled a long breath. "Okay," I reassured myself. I was on a magical roll. *Think it through.* After I had overturned the wrongful love spell, I had crafted a proper spell where Parvani, Evie, and I had listed the attributes we wished for in a boyfriend. The new incantation had worked immediately for Parvani and Evie. They'd been reunited with their true loves, Zhù and Jordan.

I sank back onto my heels. *Too bad my Mr. Right failed to materialize.*

The grimoire chirped.

I flinched like Einstein when someone squeezes his squeaky toy. "What?" I asked the spell book. For a second, I thought the grimoire appeared a little better. But it deflated and resumed its feeble death beat. Even if the rightful love spell had arrested the damage, it had been too little, too late.

Guess I'm not such a hot spell-caster after all. A fresh worry gnawed my insides. Had I made a huge mistake working magic in front of Parvani and Evie? What if word got out? Pretending to be an edgy Goth kept everyone at bay, even the school bullies, the Smash Heads. Granted Evan and Tommy weren't the brightest kids in class. At least they kept their distance. But what if I were forced out of the broom closet? The Smash Heads and everyone else would pounce.

Evie won't say anything. But Parvani might…

Fumes from *Teen Wytche* seared a raw path up my nose. Soon the degradation would be complete, and the grimoire, with all its magic and wisdom, would be lost forever. Parvani and Evie had been so confident I could save it. *I wish.* If I could work amazing magic, I'd cure Amy. Then I'd cast a brilliance spell so I wouldn't have to disguise myself. And Mr. Right would stroll into Jefferson High and fall in love with the real me.

Yeah. Right. So not going to happen.

A Note to the Readers

Thank you for reading *Spell Check*. I hope you enjoyed it! All reviews are appreciated. In addition to your social media, reviews can be posted on Goodreads or the site where you purchased this book.

Watch my website, www.AriellaMoon.com, for news on the re-release of the Teen Wytche Saga. The website also offers a glimpse into my Young Adult medieval fantasy series *The Two Realms Trilogy*, and *Two Realms Novellas*.

I love to hear from my readers. You can contact me through my website, or email me at authorariellamoon@gmail.com. And if you'd like to receive advance scoops on giveaways and upcoming releases, sign up for my newsletter through my website, like me on Facebook at http://www.facebook.com/ariellamoon.author, or follow my blog.

May all your days be magical!
~Ariella

ABOUT
ARIELLA MOON

A shaman and Wiccan priestess, Ariella Moon's life is steeped in magic. Naturally, she spent her childhood searching for a magical wardrobe that would transport her to Narnia. Extreme math anxiety, and taller students that mistook her for a leaning post, marred her youth. Despite these horrors, she graduated summa cum laude from the University of California at Davis. She lives a nearly normal life doting on her extraordinary daughter, two shamelessly spoiled dogs, and a media-shy dragon.